LOSERS AND FREAKS

LOSERS AND FREAKS

C.E. HOFFMAN

Querencia Press – Chicago IL

QUERENCIA PRESS

ISBN 978 1 959118 83 1

.

www.querenciapress.com

First Published in 2024

**Querencia Press, LLC
Chicago IL**

Printed & Bound in the United States of America

I dedicate this book to the Alberta Foundation for the Arts in thanks for their generous grant.

You have helped me feel needed, accepted, and less alone.

CONTENTS

Author's Note

This book is one big trigger warning.

i.e., it is honest, and very personal.

The suicide notes are my own—one from my first attempt that led to hospitalization in a children's psychiatric ward. The second preceded a plan thwarted by my then-boyfriend; the third failed to manifest in self-destruction.

I fret *Losers and Freaks* is too grim, despite my attempts to smatter hope and humour throughout. Moreover, I fear it's not good enough—as I fear the same about myself.

I thought my debut *Sluts and Whores* topical, whimsical, a little daring, and was surprised by the overwhelming accounts of its intensity.

If that collection was too much, what the hell is this?

Sluts and Whores was an exorcism of its own. I sought to bring a hidden side of my life to light, celebrate myself, and empower others: those brave, beautiful humans of a ubiquitous underworld. My debut dealt not only with sex work, but sexual trauma, and I didn't dare address the latter as a problem I could solve.

The same is true with *Losers and Freaks'* exhibition of mental illness.

My struggle is not backstory. It is ongoing, unreconciled, undiagnosed, and on the bad days (or months) feels untreatable. I cannot profess wisdom. Some days I can't even cope. I only hope this book will be another beacon:

I Know It Hurts; You're Not Alone.

Many (too many) struggle with mental health, and the more oppressed an individual, the less likely they will receive proper help. PoC, the trans community, neurodivergent folks, citizens of lower classes, and others suffer in ways I cannot attempt to elucidate. I can only illuminate what I've experienced, seen, or what I can imagine lies in the hearts and heads of others (and sometimes, what I've been lucky enough to have shared with me).

This is not a comprehensive collection. Some of my cruelest demons (eating disorders, self-harm) are MIA. My arms have stories of their own, but for now, these will suffice.

I hope you find comfort in this book, even if I fail to represent you exactly.

As I wrote in my grant application to the Alberta Foundation for the Arts,

"A book is a friend you carry in your pocket. I long to be a friend to many strangers."—particularly those who, like me, have always felt strange.

Like Joel of Good Charlotte says in Little Things,

"This song is dedicated to every kid who got picked last in gym class

To every kid who never had a date to no school dance

To everyone who's ever been called a freak

This is for you."

This one's for the weirdos.

Love,

C.E. Hoffman

cehoffman.net

"You can take the loser out of high school..."

—Spike, Buffy the Vampire Slayer

DELIGHTED! AND DYING*

Smile lines, cellulite—

life yet to arrive.

I'm fine, he ain't mine

Mind the gap (of time.)

Hive mind, screen bright

crying inside.

Miss him, wish I

could sleep tonight.

This was the status of my Neopet this morning. Seriously!

FIRST DATE # 5

Time moves differently in Limbo. It feels like hours, but could be days.

Either way, this is the longest date *ever*.

I'm used to guys blanking out on me. I talk a lot (too much some might say).

This one's retroactive laughter is getting to me. It takes him 1 second to compute that I, a female, have made a joke, another 2 seconds to realize said joke was funny, and by the time his brain consolidates all those stimuli into the socially acceptable reaction (laughter), my quip has long ago died on the wind, subjecting us to another round of deliciously awkward silence.

I can hardly blame him. He was a phone addict when he was alive and phone addicts are fucked in Limbo. (We wind the DJ booth with an exercise bike.) You can't find a phone until you hit Hades, and frankly, I think people are happier without them.

My date's in withdrawal. Instead of a phone, he stares at his hand, sometimes swiping his thumb against nothingness.

I want to inform him how idiotic he looks but don't want to spoil the mood.

"Hey, V!" the waiter approaches, eyes burning with sympathy. "What are we drinking?"

My date orders a Hellhound straight up.
"I invented that drink!" I tell him. "Back when I ran The Bar."

Thank god—something to talk about!

He doesn't believe me—that or, yet again, he lacks any conversational material that doesn't directly involve himself.

I log in my usual request to the waiter:

"Water?"

"Water's off."

"Dammit!"

"I have ether?"

"No thanks."

The waiter departs, soon returning with the Hellhound. My date pounds it, then orders a second, and looks at me, apparently concerned.

"Not drinking tonight?"

"I don't drink."

"Not ever?!"

"Not anymore."

"Do you smoke weed?"

"Nope."

"Meth? Nitrous oxide? Do you at least smoke pencils?"
(Drugs are limited in Limbo.)

"Not lately."

"You're totally sober?"

"Yep."

"What do you do all day?"

"Oh, you know, just curse the heavens for my sobriety."

Another joke meets an untimely demise.

I wish we could switch tables. This one is too close to the speakers, which I normally love, but it's no way to attempt conversation. The DJ is playing some amazing retro chic funk tonight: an incredible torture, since we're not allowed to dance.

That's Limbo for you: the New Bar plays the sweetest music, but dancing is forbidden. You're forced to remain seated; anything beyond bopping in place is met with immediate expulsion.

Have you ever been forced NOT to dance when the Beastie Boys are on? It's torture. Less so for me (I've never been a big dancer), but tonight even I'm feeling the pain.

Maybe it's because my date's barely looking at me. I'm second-guessing my hairstyle, my hoodie. Too slutty, or not enough? Too smart? Too stupid? Too real?

You know the night's going badly when the coke dealer on premises starts looking like a viable option. Even the guy showing us card tricks suddenly teems with appeal.

The weird thing is, Once Upon a Patriarchy, this date would have been my dream guy. He's got the beard, the laugh, the narcissist vibes. He's a DJ who travelled the world while he was alive and probably even has groupies here.

We are, in the shallowest respects, an ideal match. I, the bleach blonde pocket rocket; he, the douchebag extraordinaire. I should feel like the Queen of Saturday Night but I just feel like a loser.

I'm sick of being stared at, sick of standing out. I want to fit in! I want to belong!

I'm scared I'll never belong anywhere.

Once I had friends. Once I even had a future.

I blew it.

zoomwoomwooom...

Something whizzes into the room. It's a tiny white turtle with butterfly wings. It shimmers, leaving a shiny dust trail behind it.

It's a red herring! These little guys are messengers from the Powers That May Be. They recruit Observers, Guardian Angels, etc.

This is it! My death will never be the same! I don't need to be normal. I'm special! I'm picked! I'm...

The red herring zoomwooms over to my date, whispers in his ear, and woomzooms away.

You're fucking kidding me!

"*You?*" I nearly scream. "*You've* been chosen to go topside?"

"Huh? Oh, no. I hired a red herring as my messenger service. How else can I text people down here?"

"Oh. What was the "text"?"

"Oh. Haha. Yeah. I invited another girl. She just got here."

"...What?"

"Haha. Yeah."

"That's... awkward."

"Haha. Yeah. Be cool, okay?"

Be cool? He asked another girl on our date, and he's asking *me* to be cool?

He stands up, suppressing the urge to groove.

"I'm going to get another drink. Don't move!"

He's not going to get another drink! He's going to see his *other* date, and try to discern the best way to juggle us both. Like we're conflicting subjects on his timetable. Like we're two bitches he arranged to walk the same night!

My dead body is bathed in ice. I have finally learned to identify this emotion: it's called anger. And I hate it.

I would kill almost anyone, including myself (again!) to never feel this way.

How amazing that a veritable stranger, one I'm not even interested in, could hurt me so much.

It only now occurs to me that he hasn't asked me about music all night. Everyone, dead or alive, knows I breathe, eat, shit music (I don't breathe or shit anymore, but the point stands). That he should sit here for so long, staring at his hand more than he's looked at me and not even ask me about DJing—a passion we purportedly share—is beyond humiliating.

Furthermore, I can't figure out just how insulted I should be about him asking out a girl halfway through our date. Should I be flattered that I was his Plan A? Or insulted that I missed out on the nightshift? After all, the one on the nightshift is the one you're hoping to sleep with.

It's not all bad, really. The DJ's on fire (literally) and I met some nice girls, though of course none of them were gay.

He comes back 10 minutes later (must have been a big drink).

Drunks are great at rearranging their memories. He's probably fixing the story as we speak, fashioning me as the dumb blonde bitch, he as the innocent.

"It's getting late," that's my hint.

"Oh, you want me to get you a cab? Or, you know, a bike?"

I almost take up his offer.

Then I remember I can't leave.

This is not an especially momentous epiphany in Limbo. Lots of people start off stuck, and lots stay that way. There was a perpetual line outside The Club until it got torn apart by zombies. There's a house party that forever parties on, independent of time zones or holidays.

The New Bar is special because anyone can leave but me. It is my personal, pretty prison: penance for that one slip, and now here I am, doomed to a leaden eternity of exceptionally bad first dates.

I am stuck in a literal cage. My table is surrounded by locks and bars: the endangered blonde on display. I have the seat closest to the stage, but that's as much as a punishment as anything—to be so close and so far from the DJ booth, my salvation just out of reach, my rightful throne forever usurped.

There was a time I would have thrown my drink, glass and all, in my date's face. Those days are gone. It may feel badass in the moment, but only causes problems.

I'm sick of drama. I'm sick of being everyone's jailbait and/or crazy chick. I want to be taken seriously, but that's never going to happen.

Poison is the classiest way to end this date.

Killing him might be overkill. Nobody knows where you go when you die twice. It'll definitely screw over that probation I've been vying for, but who cares? Limbo ain't any better on the outside. The only difference is these bars are visible.

It's not all bad. Really.

At least I've got music.

SUICIDE NOTE #1

Dear Diary,

well im not sure what the date is. i know it hasn't been long since my last entry. i know it's late at night. a night that seems like any other nite. but tonite is special. yes, i am happy. why? that's my secret, and i swore not to tell.

im not quite sure, but im hopeful. very hopeful.

my mouth feels dry. im tired.

think ill go 2 sleep now.

SCHRODINGER'S CATS

Waking up with her was wonderful.

She insisted on touching only after she went to the washroom, so I killed time with a bong hit on the balcony.

"Say, where's the cat?" I asked.

"Oh." she said through the door. "Gone."

My tabby rubbed up on my ankle.

"Ha-ha. Very funny. She's right here."

"Oh." she exited the washroom with The Acid House, toilet bowl mid-flush. "No. That's a decoy."

"Ha-ha. Very funny. What did you do with the real one?"

"She wanted out in the middle of the night. What was I supposed to do?"

She was serious.

"Yes, I'm serious! The cat wanted out, so I brought her onto the balcony, but then there was this portal…"

"Portal?"

"A small one! I didn't think both of us could even fit. But, when she went, I went too."

"Where?"

"Oh." she put the bookmark in her book. "Some alternate dimension."

"What?"

"It's not my fault! It's extremely easy to lose cats in alternate dimensions!"

"So…" a chill ran up my leg. "This cat is…?"

"Not your cat. Not strictly speaking." she handed me my coffee (one cream, one sugar).

I took my coffee, gave her a kiss, and headed to the balcony.

"Say, where you going?" she asked.

"To find that damn portal and get my cat back!"

"Oh." she walked onto the balcony with me. The air was crisp. The day had begun. "Are you sure you'll fit? You're taller than me."

"I'll make do."

"What about the *other* cat?" she indicated the alternate feline, who had curled up in my tabby's bed.

"It's not the same!" I insisted.

"Why not? If this cat knows you, and loves you, how is it any different from the original?"

A chill went through my heart.

"Are you…?"

"Not strictly. But what's it matter if it feels right?"

Her hand found mine, and it fit.

I AIN'T NO
ALBAE GALLINAE FILIUS

Once upon a Patriarchy in the Big City, 28 years before its revolution and sequential decay, two strippers stole a baby.

These were no ordinary strippers. (Is any stripper ordinary?)

Chevon, the white girl, had werewolf blood. The Black girl, Aphrodite (Aph for short), was part pixie (on her mom's side).

By no means do I want to stereotype, but this mystical lineage should illuminate their personalities. If not, refer to the dialogue.

"Jesus, Aph." Chevon lifted her butt to accommodate a fart. "Quit playing with that thing."

"It's not a thing," corrected Aphrodite, "it's a baby!"

"I mean the radio! I can't hear myself think!"

Reluctant, Aph ejected her Parliament/Funkadelic tape. In her lap, the infant gurgled in vain protest.

She whispered him a tune,

"We got a real type of thing going down, getting down

there's a whole lot of rhythm going round…"

"You call that a lullaby?" Chevon lit a Belmont cig without rolling down the window; Aphrodite did it for her.

"Why not? Funk is good for you!"

"That kid," Chevon pointed her cigarette; ash fell dangerously close to the baby blankets, "will not grow up listening to funk."

"Doesn't matter! Music is universal. Genres are just… languages."

"Poetic. Hang on, I gotta piss."

Chevon pulled over their 1992 Chevrolet Corsica (silver, stolen) and proceeded to drop trou.

She was mid-stream when the demons came.

***

Prophecies are tricky (any Harry Potter fan will tell you this). Our attempted avoidance often makes prophecies pass in the first place. We'd be better off not-knowing, but humanity is nothing if not curious. Same goes for other sentient beings.

I presume you know the song Fortunate Son by Credence Clearwater Revival? One of the best songs of 1969, in my opinion, and it has competition.

It is also considered the most accurate prophecy written after 1493.

I won't waste time dissecting every allegedly prophetic line. The only detail of importance for this story is many magically-diverse folk were convinced the sacred son in question was none other than the six-month old baby Chevon and Aphrodite had absconded with.

The demons landed their helicopter next to Chevon's Chevy.

By the time she zipped up, it was too late.

That is, too late to negotiate.

"Bastards!" Chevon howled.

The demons (or bastards) in question were handsome, tall, and white—the preferred human suit for any hellion working topside.

The tallest, handsomest, and whitest aimed his phallic gun at Chevon's head. His "superior" demon Fic was supposed to lead this operation, but of course ditched, leaving this "inferior" demon, Pelf, to the dirty work.

"Hand over the kid."

"Did you or did you not hear me howl 'Bastards'?"

If Chevon was a target, Pelf hit the bulls-eye. She splattered against the car hood; Aphrodite went, "Oh geez."

Pelf approached the passenger side, and took new aim.

"I hate repeating myself."

Chevon slammed him on the pavement.

"So do I!" she snarled, and struggled to dig the bullet from her forehead. "Didn't even bring silver bullets. Idiots!"

Aphrodite leaned on the horn.

"Get in the car, dammit!"

Pelf's lackeys made Swiss cheese of their ride, to which Chevon replied,

"Get out of the car, dammit!"

Chevon shielded Aph and the baby, both of whom were more vulnerable to regular bullets than she. Together, they dodged the onslaught, and made it behind the vehicle.

"Oh geez," Aph lamented, "my tape's still in there!"

"I don't care about the bloody tape! You know what you've got to do."

"It's not going to work!"

"C'mon, you have to!"

"For gosh sake, Chev!"

"Ugh. Fine!"

Chevon picked up Aphrodite, Aphrodite picked up the baby, and off they went.

***

When they reached The Nursery, their roly-poly captive needed changing. Chevon obliged, but only after lighting another Belmont.

"That was close," she commented as she wiped the baby clean.

Aph checked the other babies (twelve in all) whilst fretting,

"We shouldn't have left that tape."

"Enough about the tape!"

"Music is more powerful than you think!"

"Blah blah." Chevon tickled the newest baby's feet, and pinned his fresh diaper shut. "We're fine. We're safe. This was the last baby that could possibly be the AGF." she lifted it into the light. "Funny. They all look so normal."

"It's *not* fine. We're *not* safe."

Chevon shrugged, cig dangling from her lip.

"I don't see why we have to worry."

Are there last words any more famous?

CRASH!—Pelf's gang came through the roof (without even knocking!). The babies cried and coughed. Aph shielded those she could reach, and Chevon held their latest addition tight.

If she had to fight one-handed, so be it.

"Pixies always leave a trace on their possessions." Pelf crushed Aphrodite's tape in his fingers. "Idiots."

Chevon warned her friend,

"Don't say you told me so!"

"Let's try this again." Pelf's greedy eyes needled the baby. "Give me the kid, or we make the rest of these little mutants into a bonfire."

"You just try it!" Chevon dared, but the dare was weak, and Pelf knew it.

"Fucking good guys. You're so easy to manipulate."

Pelf extended his arms longer and longer. His palms grew wider and wider. They surrounded the baby boy, ironically asleep on Chevon's chest. Chevon wouldn't let go.

"Please, Chev." Aph bit her lip. "Think of the others."

Chevon relented with a growl. Pelf laughed, "Down, girl."

He tucked the baby under his snazzy leather trench coat (demons love dressing like Nazis).

The demons returned to their helicopter; Chevon kicked a chair in defeat.

"He's right." Chevon teared. "Goodness makes you weak."

"That's what they want you to think," cooed Aphrodite. "We can still make this right. We can do the right thing."

Chevon wiped snot on her arm.

"Lucky us."

Aphrodite hugged her friend's waist.

"We know one thing for sure." Chevon narrowed her eyes, "That kid is the one."

***

"How do we find them?" wondered the half-werewolf.

"Don't worry about that," comforted the half-pixie. "Demons leave a trace of their own."

"I'm not following."

"C'mon, Chev—sniff them out!"

"I didn't even think of that!"

Chevon breathed long and deep.

"I can't get anything. Must be the cigarettes."

"Ugh. Never mind. We'll do it the old fashioned way."

"Yay! Are you finally going to fly?"

"No, Chevon! I've told you a million times I can't. Human bodies are too heavy."

"Yeah, well," Chevon shrugged, "our bodies aren't strictly human."

Aphrodite looked at her hands, and the nails she had to file daily lest they turn into pixie talons.

"Not strictly."

***

The demon's lair was on the North Side (demons love luxury). It was one of those huge estates that have their own golf course attached. And it was on this terrain of privileged greens that Chevon and Aphrodite had their third standoff after arriving the old-fashioned way (by way of housing listings, and bus).

Seeing as the demons jumped them, threw them on their backs and threatened to douse Chevon with moon powder, it's safe to say they began at a disadvantage.

"I told you we should have come from the front!" Chevon admonished. "Now we have to surrender!"

"Chevon, it's just moon powder!"

"Not to me it isn't! Do something! Fly us!"

"For the last time, you know I can't!"

"Well," Chev cowered, "do something!"

"Ugh. Fine!"

"Well?" the demon shook his vial of foreboding crystals.

Aphrodite replied with her version of a lullaby.

"We're gonna turn this mother out!

We're gonna turn this mother out!"

Fun fact: funk is pure joy distilled into audible vibrations. i.e., it is death for demons.

They dropped their guns, covered their ears. Their human masks slipped, giving a glimpse of the anguish underneath.

"Make it stop, make it stop!"

Aphrodite upped the ante—and the volume.

"We want the funk! Give up the funk!
We need the funk! Gotta have that funk…"

The demons ran. Our proud pixie produced a grin so grand Chevon had to return her own lopsided smile.

"I TOLD you music was powerful!"

"In the hands of a pixie, maybe." Chevon rolled to her feet. "C'mon. You may have saved us, but we still have to save that baby."

***

This lair had a portal to Hell installed in the basement.

In lieu of your usual entertainment centre or foosball table, you had something resembling the heart of a volcano, complete with jagged cliffs and threatening liquids.

Pelf held the baby over the abyss while blasting Fortunate Son from several strategically-placed boomboxes. Meanwhile, his remaining backup chanted (in Latin!), creating quite the cacophony:

"Albae Gallinae Filius

Bestium et interitum

Usque ad infinitum…"

"Some folks are born silver spoon in hand

Lord, don't they help themselves..."

"What are they doing?" Aphrodite worried.

"Call it a creepy baptism. Like, creepier than usual." Chevon peered out from their ledge. "They're going to throw him into that hellwater, thus activating the prophecy."

"That's horrible!"

"No shit. What are we gonna do about it?"

Aphrodite brightened.

"Fly!"

Chevon glowered.

"You told me you can't!"

"I can't! I'm too heavy! But that baby might be light enough."

Pelf and the baby were a few stories above them, the water some stories below. If lucky, Aphrodite's pixie magic would catch the innocent before it hit hellwater.

All the while, CCR protested in song.

"Some folks inherit star-spangled eyes..."

Pelf held the bairn by its foot; even then, it didn't cry.

"They send you down to war..."

WOOSH!- the little tumbled into darkness.
"And when you ask them, How much should we give?"

ZING!- Aphrodite aimed blindly.

"They only answer, More, more, more!"

The baby hung mid-air, on its belly, dangling an inch above the water's oily surface.

"It ain't me, it ain't me

I ain't no military son, no

It ain't me, It ain't me..."

FLASH!- Pelf struck the baby with a purple bolt.

"I ain't no fortunate one!"

"No!"

Aphrodite fought back. The magics clashed: Aphrodite's happy pink and Pelf's noxious purple, with the baby suspended between the beams, sinking and floating all at once.

"Did it touch the water?" Chevon shrieked.

"Let the baby go!" screamed Pelf.

"Shut up!" Aphrodite yelled- to whom, it wasn't clear.

Magic is a funny thing. (Any readers of C. S. Lewis will concur.) One can never plan for magic any more than one can plan for death. You can try, but you'll always look like an idiot.

In this case, love was stronger than hate. It doesn't always work that way, but this time, it did.

The tension snapped; Pelf fell over, Aphrodite fell back. The kidlet flew, and Chevon dived for it.

"Chevon, no!" cried her friend.

Too late. Chevon caught the baby, but for her own body there would be no such protection. She landed square in the centre of the abyss, but it wasn't as deep as she expected. Hellish liquid lapped at her hips, and she held the baby overhead to wade to shore.

Pelf screamed so loud he muted the music. He shot purple, orange, red and green bolts. They bounced off the walls. They made sparks, then tidal waves.

"We've got to get out of here!" Chevon screamed.

"No shit!" Aph screamed back, dragging her friend (and the baby) to safety.

The lair collapsed from its own corruption. They got out in time to watch hellwater gurgle up from the grass, then sink back, satisfied with this sacrifice.

"Did it get him? Did it get him?" Chevon repeated, while her own body was charred with otherworldly tar.

"What about you?"

"Forget me! Make sure he's okay!"

Aphrodite checked the babe from head to toe, and winced at a certain discovery.

"Um, sorta."

"What do you mean, sort of?!"

"Well," Aphrodite looked embarrassed. "You know that moment when they say, It's a boy! or, you know, not?"

"I hope there's a point to this."

"There is a point! I mean, it's that… part."

Chevon, though shaky, sat up.

"Are you telling me his little baby penis…?"

"…Got dipped in hellwater. Yes."

"Well," Chevon examined her own body. "He got off better than me."

"Does it hurt?"

Chevon touched her legs in surprise.

"No, actually."

They watched the black disappear into Chevon's skin, and so too did the baby's nethers fade back to their original hue.

They waited for hellfire, brimstone, or at least boils.

None came.

"Well, well." Chevon poked the baby's cheeks. "You really are a fortunate son!"

"Alright," said a voice, "Hand over the kid."

***

"Not again!" Aph moaned, and joined Chevon in poking a baby cheek. "You really are trouble, little one!"

"Well worth it." Chevon rejoined, and shouted to the darkness, "Go ahead, try and take him! I bathe in hellwater, bitch!"

"Such language." a figure appeared from darkness, and shook pixie dust off their coat.

Chevon greeted the person with,

"Oh great. An HSW."

The Heavenly Social Worker straightened their lapel.

"No need for unpleasantries. You simply must return the baby to its home. *All* the babies." they added with an admonitory stare.

"That's gonna be awkward." Chevon mumbled.

Aph protested,

"Not this one! He only caught a bit of hellwater, but…"

"None of this is your decision! We are not the makers of destiny. We can only follow it."

"Bullshit!" grumbled Chev. "Destiny's all we make ourselves."

"Enough philosophy! Do what you're told!"

"But," Aph cuddled the little one, "someone needs to look out for him!"

"Don't worry." the HSW prepared to teleport. "Someone will."

***

35

In a 1988 Volkswagen Cabriolet (also silver, also stolen), our would-be wonders returned the baby to its mother, an Asian lady who was busy nursing the baby boy's twin sister.

"Here," Chevon offered the wee one. "We sorta borrowed him."

The mother accepted the precious cargo, somewhere between elated and terrified.

"So, could you maybe fax us if he starts killing things with his penis…?" Chevon was silenced by Aphrodite's boot.

"We should go!" Aphrodite grinned so wide you could almost see her pixie teeth, but on their way out, both hesitated.

"Just wondering…" Chevon turned around.

Aphrodite completed the thought,

"What do you call him?"

The mother looked down at her beautiful baby boy.

"Ezekiel Simon Bowery. But his daddy calls him Ez."

STOCKHOLM SYNDROME:
A LOVE STORY

I came willingly.

That's what he says.

The singing walls make it hard to think straight. Same with the never-ending waterfall of whiskey.

Where are my sleeping chambers…? This place is too big to be this drunk in. (Too many stairs.)

God bless my poor head. Hammerhead sharks hammered nails and…

He's been kind tonight. You'd think kindness would be a relief, but nowadays I count down the minutes until he unleashes the beast.

Dancing used to calm him down, but he complains his knees are too sore.

The fire spits licks of orange across the carpet. Is that my head spinning, or is it the room?

Head, meet floor.

Boom.

"Tut tut." sings the kettle. "Tut tut."

"Don't judge me!" I wipe my mouth on the bearskin rug, which rumbles in protest.

Ketty rolls my way, somehow managing not to slosh all over. I wish she'd teach me how not to make such a mess.

"You've been bathing in single malt again."

"Not intentionally." I'd get up, but why bother? "Just fell in, that's all."

"Mhm." can she smell me? I hope not. "Let's get you cleaned up. He'll be expecting you for dinner."

***

The world is too intense. Like that wallpaper. I'll never get used to it.

My wardrobe helps me dress, mostly 'cause I'm too sauced to do it myself. She's still trying to get me to wear frills; I'm almost depressed enough to give in.

I sneak a sip from my favourite flask.

"Tut tut." says Ketty.

"Mind your own business!"

"You sure you don't want to try a corset?" Coddy coos, cornice all up like concerned eyebrows.

***

The dining room is dimly lit (thank fuck.) The candles wink while they melt down into goop that'll crust and peel off the candelabras. Do they feel? Does it hurt? Why can't I hear them scream?

He's at the head of the table, like always, almost tall enough to upset the chandelier (who gets upset easily.)

Is my lover/captor/whatever handsome? Usually. It's weird being attracted to someone so scary. Do I love him despite his monstrous qualities, or because of them?

Do I love him?

"Good evening, Evalina."

"Leander, I've told you, just call me Eva."

"I cannot permit it. One thing you've taught me, Evalina, is good manners."

"True. May I join you?"

"Be my guest."

My chair scuttles back to let me sit. Head swinging, I almost slip, but the seat catches me before my date notices.

I hear the dishes humming in the kitchen. Plates waltz, forks river dance.

"Shall we start with some asparagus soup?" this is a bid to please me: when I first moved in, it was roast beef 24/7. (Very, very rare.)

I imagine the milky-green liquid bubbling in my mouth.

I don't think I can keep down dinner.

He needs me to be ecstatic over the upcoming asparagus soup. Anything less than elation will be considered hostile. Unfortunately for him, and particularly for me, I am too preoccupied with my cranial merry-go-round to invoke anything beyond polite complacency.

"Yes, that sounds nice."

Like magic, his fuse is lit.

"Why do you have to punish me like this?"

"I'm not punishing anyone, Leander. I'm just tired."

"Of this? Of us?"

"That's not what I meant!"

Who do I have to kill to hear about the wine selection?

"You came here of your own free will."

"I know, I know…" I try to look outside, but can't see the stars for the prison bars.

"Do you, though?" his eyes wrinkle. "Lately, it seems like you only blame me."

"Can we not do this tonight?"

"I treat you well. I give you everything you could ever need. And you love me, don't you?"

I stare hard into his eyes, flashing back to all those times I willed his inner prince appear, and was met only with dark pupils, and darker irises.

"Of course I do. Which is why you don't have to be so possessive. For example, you could, I don't know, let me go outside?"

"I'm not possessive, I'm protective. There's a difference. Besides, this spell's taken a little longer than we expected. Removing it, I mean."

He stares down at his big mitts, slowly dropping his fists on the tablecloth.

"You promised you'd stay with me 'til the end."

Did I?

There's more things I need to know, more things I ought to ask.

But I keep getting lost in his eyes.

***

Certain rooms are off limits. Certain towers, certain wings.

I used to go exploring; he stomped out that habit.

How did I feel when I first arrived with my big bag of books and big head full of dreams? I try to remember what I thought when I first laid eyes upon him and realized I'd been catfished beyond belief.

The general consensus is I chose to stay, for the good of my family, or civilization, or something, but I'm starting to wonder if I ever had a choice.

Maybe I'm not a princess, but a sacrifice.

"Arms up!" Cloddy pulls my dress over my head.

I'm wilted like those sad bouquets the garden shovels bury in the backyard. I struggle into a slip and crawl onto my mattress which has apparently transformed into a water bed.

Magic, magic, everywhere, and not a drop of relief.

I need some sleep…

RING! RING!

"That'll be the Master, dearie. Shall I fetch your slippers?"

Fuck sake.

***

Ketty follows me down the stairs, nipping my ankle like a wayward dog.

"Why didn't you let Coddy get you a nightgown? It's freezing!"

"I'm sick of being waited on hand and foot!"

"You wouldn't know where your foot was if we didn't show you!"

"Shut up, Ketty!"

"You listen to me, Missy. You are up to your neck in Glenfiddich. Myself and the other dining ware are concerned…"

"Ketty, I told you to shut up!"

"Who are you talking to?" Leander comes around the corner, all massive shadows and imposing bulk, making me feel smaller than I actually am.

In tandem, we eye the kettle sitting at my foot on the stairwell. I scoop it up with what I hope is a breezy laugh.

"No one! That is, myself."

"Were you talking to that teapot?"

"It's a kettle. And no I was not."

"You're going crazy!"

"That is *not* a gentlemanly comment."

He composes himself.

"Forgive me. I was hoping you might read to me tonight."

"Sure." I venture into the second parlour room. "But nothing French."

Sometimes his smile is my lifeline. My body bends before him, a leaf in a dust storm. It's easy to give in, at first. Then the consequences pile up, and before you know it, you're Atlas, with no way to shrug off the world.

Isn't love supposed to be a fairytale?

Is it really as bad as I think it is? He barely yells anymore. His beastliness is more subtle, perhaps more insidious. Maybe he doesn't mean to hurt me. Maybe he doesn't know.

We try some Orlando, but the swirly sentences refuse capture from my clumsy jaw. My brain can't get a grip. I keep wondering how long it's been, how old I've gotten (Leander's covered all the mirrors.) How pale must I be? When was the last time I smelled fresh air?

I try again,

"I'd really like to go outside."

"You know I'd die without you." He means it. Literally.

"I'm sure you wouldn't die if I went around the block!"

"Do you remember what happened last time?"

"Vaguely."

"I simply won't allow it. I love you too much. And you love me."

"Okay, well, how about hiring some people? It's such a huge place for just the two of us."

"I don't want anyone else around to divide your attentions."

"Seriously?" I shouldn't talk when I'm this drunk. "What, you worried I'm going to fall for my whipping boy?"

His eyes flash in lieu of a roar. My hunger for his hands transforms into horror. (It's getting harder to tell the two apart.)

"It… it was a joke, okay?"

"Don't joke about things like that."

Maybe I shouldn't talk at all.

***

What was she, anyway? A fairy, an angel, a witch?

She's all I remember from the first night I was here. I was up in my room, cursing and crying when, out of nowhere, light flooded the air, and there she was, so perfect, so beautiful, so far away from me.

What did she say? Something about how if I loved him for who he was, he would become the person he was meant to be.

She neglected to mention a few things.

Like how learning to love a monster can rob the best years of your life. Or how putting up with his daily abuses will invariably lead to substance abuse. Or, how the more you put up with, the more he realizes he can get away with.

I've forgotten what it's like to have an opinion without causing an argument. If I don't assent, we fight.

These days, I'm not in the mood for prostration.

"When are you going to drop this?"

"When am I going to get to go outside? And can you please let me sleep at night? No more late summonings. I mean it."

"You want to go? Then go!"

"Very funny. You know I can't get through unless you lift the bars!"

I never knew a laugh could hurt so much. He flings open those huge medieval doors with a flick of his wrist, and there's no gates, no barricades, not even a moat like I remember. The air is shrill with cold, dead night, and the woods ahead glimmer with unspoken secrets.

Leander moves behind me, but it feels like he's in my way. He towers over me, but I can still feel his breath on my neck as he whispers,

"You're not going crazy- you're already insane! Those bars are in your head. You could leave anytime you want. You don't want to."

I want to.

I don't know how.

It's there. Open. Right in front of me. My freedom, my future, my everything.

Why can't I go?

Why don't I leave?

He's right. Even if I didn't arrive willingly, even if I didn't want to stay, I still have a choice. Everyone does.

I need a drink.

***

Maybe he doesn't want me sober. Why else would he have installed all those Scotch fountains and Bourbon waterfalls?

Maybe the only way I can escape from his demon is if I control my own first.

The world can be intense AND beautiful. I can find my feet again, and put one in front of the other.

The trees are bare. Snow is coming. I take my book bag downstairs, and of course find Leander by the fire, flipping through Voltaire.

When I first arrived, he used his library for kindling.

Maybe I did him some good.

It wasn't always terrible. Like, back when he still let me outside, we had a snowball fight. I landed one right in his face! It was the first time I made him laugh.

I would have given anything to keep feeling that.

"Lea?"

"Evalina?"

"I'm leaving."

"Not this again."

"I mean it this time. I could have tried to sneak away but… you deserve better than that."

Leander closes the book; the pages hiccough.

"So, you're, what, out of love with me?"

"No. I don't think that part of the spell will ever be broken. But I can't waste my life waiting for you to change."

The monster's let loose. He roars like the good old days, and throws Voltaire in the fire. The cover's face smiles in its destruction. Why won't it show fear? Why won't it fucking scream?

"You want to go, fine. But I'll die if you stay away. Even if you leave, you have to come back."

"I can't keep sacrificing my own life so you can keep yours! That's not love, okay? And if it is, I don't want the fairy tale anymore."

He's on my tail, smelling of violence, claws casting a shadow on my heart.

The doors feel far away.

"You can't say no to this. To me. This is destiny."

He grabs hold of me, and won't let go.

I used to love feeling his weight. There used to be something exciting in knowing I couldn't escape.

He expects me to be weak, like always. Weak from the booze, the stress, from this wicked sexy roller coaster I lined up for every day.

What he doesn't know is I've been off whiskey for weeks. I've been back to reading my own books.

I'm becoming the person I could be.

His paws can tear, lacerate. He can rip me up, if he wants.

I can't fight him alone.

My cutlery buddies descend from the ceiling. Vases smash, plates riot. The vacuum cleaner soups up his hooves; the curtains cover his eyes as the perfect blindfold. Ketty steams up the place, and I wish I had time to thank her, but all she says is,

"Go!!!!"

God bless my clear head. I finally remember all of it: my father, my sisters, the ships wrecked at sea, and the single rose that ruined everything.

Most importantly, I know how to get back home.

I've learned the end to this story, and it's not what people think.

The monster never becomes a man. You can teach him to read or eat with a spoon, but he'll never shed his pelt, and you'll never touch the shiny prince within-

if he's even in there at all.

POSTER OF A GIRL

—Inspired by a chapter in Portrait of a Lady by Henry James. Some dialogue and descriptions have been lifted from the original text

You may have heard writers argue the villa was "long and rather blank-looking", but in actuality, that house hosted more colour and horror than any of its occupants would admit.

I am sure you heard about the girl. You may even remember what they said about her hair, and where it fell, or how carefully she examined her father's latest watercolour.

(In case you've forgotten, her hair was sand blonde, and would have grazed her shoulders had it not been held back with the rest of her personality.)

Her father smoked on the couch, and asked his daughter if she liked the painting.

"Yes, Papa. Did you make it yourself?"

"Certainly I made it. Don't you think I'm clever?"

One might give the father the benefit of the doubt, and assume this comment was made in jest, but anyone could see he all at once sought authority over and approval from his daughter, Pansy, who gave him all this and more.

She agreed,

"Yes, Papa, very clever." then added a risky afterthought, "I also have learned to make pictures."

The nuns observed Pansy from the corner, the father only scarcely perceptible to them. Mother Catherine and Sister Sarah appeared devoted to the child, and would have confirmed this if you asked.

It was a bright day in May (May 1st, as the record stands), but a chill persisted.

Everyone watched the girl. Pansy pretended not to notice, and walked the room's length, hands behind her back as she examined the books, but her father knew she would not take one unless asked.

The nuns had made her into a good Christian, and a very good girl.

"Do you draw at school, Pansy?" he asked too late to be sincere, but his daughter answered with grace,

"I've brought very many; they're in my trunk."

"She draws very… carefully." Mother Catherine remarked.

"I'm glad to hear it." the father reclined. "And how is her health?"

They spoke as if Pansy were absent, but Pansy was used to it.

"Good," began the younger Sister, "but I think she has finished growing. She will remain… not big."

Pansy's father remained at ease.
"I'm not sorry. I prefer women like books- very good and not too long. What do you see in the garden?" this last query was directed to Pansy, who had travelled to the window, and while her nose nearly pressed the glass, she dared not raise a hand.

"Flowers." her voice was almost a whisper. "So many flowers."

"Not many good ones, though." replied the father. "That's the problem. Good flowers are so rare."

"Yes, Papa." Pansy concurred.

Her beloved patriarch addressed the nuns,

"I sent you my daughter to see what you'd make of her. She's perfect!"

They nodded in quiet agreement. The girl in question nodded too, for it seemed the thing to do.

"Would you two like to see the garden?" he offered. "Perhaps you might pick some bouquets before your departure."

Pansy, usually so proper, managed to request,

"Can't I too?"

"When I tell you." said the father. He and the nuns exchanged glances. Perhaps seeing the flowers had been too much for her.

This is where facts get fuzzy. Other accounts presume upon Pansy's peaceable nature; they make no allowance for her vicissitudes of spirit. Further writings claim Pansy was glad to receive another visitor, who we will call Madame M., but if one looked closely, you would have seen her bottom lip quiver.

They passed what could have been observed as pleasantries, and Pansy's father offered to show the nuns the garden. Pansy followed, but Madam M. asked, or perhaps instructed,

"Stay with me."

Pansy's eyes welled, yet for all her protests, she obeyed.

"Can I not go out with Mama Catherine?"

Madame M. smiled, but her eyes were cold.

"It is better if you stay."

"Alright." Pansy nodded. "I'll stay."

"It is good that they taught you to obey."

"Yes, Madame."

Pansy's father returned with a tiny bouquet of red roses, which he extended to Madame M.

Pansy returned to her father's picture, which may have suffered more critique had Pansy been permitted honesty.

"I hoped you would meet me in Rome." the Madame berated the Mister.

"Sound reasoning. But this is not the first time I've acted outside of your calculations."

"I think you positively perverse." she said it like a compliment.

He was a little wary.

"If we're going to discuss this, we should have her leave the room."

"Do you want me to go?" wondered Pansy.

"Let her stay." said Madame.

Pansy offered,

"If you like, I won't listen!"

The father changed his mind.

"You may stay. You won't understand what we're saying."

This was a lie. Pansy understood too much, especially with her sedative wearing off. Her father knew this, and willed the nuns to return. Perhaps they'd become complacent. Perhaps they'd forgotten what she was.

It was impossible not to fall in love with Pansy. She was exceptional, no matter her state. Hadn't everything he'd done been to protect her? Like the original documents concerning this case, Pansy's father liked to simplify.

Pansy paced faster and faster. Just when her father was about to breach panic, Madame M. snapped,

"Enough, child!"
The action abated, and Pansy was perfect again.

"Yes, Madame."

Madame M. and Pansy's father relaxed, now free to focus on more important matters.

"Well then, what are your plans for her?" the lady inquired. "We can, I assume, consider the test a success."

"Call it a test? This is my daughter!" the man insisted, then relented, "And she is nothing short of a success."

"This is her first visit since…?"

"Yes." he cast the girl a glance, relieved to see she was preoccupied with an ornament on the side table. "Of course, she'll have to stay inside until it's perfected. But in time, she'll be able to move back in with me."

A little voice said,

"N…o."

The nuns returned in time to witness this dramatic event. Both dropped their bouquets. The whole room took a breath. Everything froze, then came back to life for Pansy's dear old dad to ask,

"What did you say?"

The sweet girl's lips formed around the contraband word,

"N…no."

The father's eyes snapped to the nuns, in hot pursuit for someone to blame.

"Which of you taught her that word?!"

"We would never!" insisted Sister Sarah. "It must be left over from before…"

Pansy's eyes widened, and her voice rose.

"N…no!"

"The sedative!" Madame M. ordered. "Quickly!"

It was she who produced the syringe from Mother Catherine's bag; the nuns were too hesitant; they suffered the sin of doubt, and the even worse sin of hope. Hope that Pansy would be fine. Hope that everything would go back to normal. Hope that they'd never have to drug that dear child again.

Madame grabbed Pansy by the arms, who was now fit enough for a struggle.

"No!"

The syringe plunged into Pansy's bicep; she wilted.

"N…o…"

"Shh, good girl." her father was on his knees, petting her hair. Then, to the nuns, "Will that be enough?"

"Why, you've emptied the syringe!" the Sister shuddered. "She barely needs more than a drop to hold her under!"

"Well," unapologetic, Madame M. left Pansy crumpled on the floor, "she'll be easier to drive back this way."

Pansy's head threatened to fall from her neck. Her eyes steadied, first focusing on the floor, then landing on Madame M.

"No! No no no no no no no!" the dissension returned like a chatter in Pansy's teeth, and with every "No!" came wind crashing on windows, lightning crashing at the door, books crashing to the floor.

Everyone in this room knew the power of No, and the incredible magic it could wield. As soon as Pansy was born, it was obvious she was special, and everyone knew she couldn't stay that way.

"No!" Pansy's whisper grew into a scream. Crystal shattered, spitting shards. Lightning spun about her head: a new halo. The wind lifted her from the floor like she had wings.

All those well-meaning monsters cowered before her, and as you have read, no accounts include what came next.

One thing was certain: Pansy was perfect again.

SHUT UP

She finds the map. "You Are Here." Here she is. Chewed-down
nails and a feverish countenance.

She checks her watch. Two hours to kill. The watch reminds her,

"Tick. Tick. Tick!"

Right floor? Yes. Room 383. No point heading in yet. (Nobody wants to be
that eager.)

One day she'll stop relying on maps and find her own way. Today is
practice: she will wander the library.

It's her first time on campus.

Creeeeeak. The doors need olive oil. The building is old enough to be in
disrepair and new enough to be ugly. The shelves are pointedly unromantic.
No nymphs whisper in these walls. Walt Whitman dropped no pens here.

The lace on her boots whistles down the aisle,

"Zing! Zing!"

She immediately feels conspicuous. Books stare, and students, too. Could
she walk any quieter, please? If only nobody noticed her at all.

"QUIET STUDY." shouts a sign. Ah. This awkward silence is not hers alone. The silence is a choice. A moral. A mandate.

Of course, she needs to sneeze. Hold it back! Think of something!

Her nose cries,

"Itch! Itch! ITCH!"

It passes. She checks her watch.

One hour and fifty-eight minutes.

She'd go outside, but it's cold, and her boots are cheap. She'd call a friend, but her friends are yet to be made.

(It's her first time on campus.)

She tries a smile: smiles are quiet. Her target readjusts their gaze.

One only hears the rare turn of page, so many absorbed by their screens while books look on jealously. Her jacket's zipper gives her away; she blushes all the way into the stacks.

At least the books are welcoming. They grin like eager old maids. Her fingers tease spines untouched. She dare not open any.

Swish!- something (someone?) steals her periphery.

Swish!- again! Someone's skirt! A laugh?

She listens hard to cut through the silence.

She follows the bread crumbs of sound.

"Pss!"- like someone coaxing a cat.

A brush. A touch.

A moan?

She walks further and further in, boots softly scudding tarnished carpet. If a fire alarm sounded, she wouldn't know the way out.

There they are. A girl. A boy. Kisses buried among the fall of the Roman Empire.

Back here, dust sings low tones on old tomes; faint notes of sunlight harmonize.

Their kisses are too deep to make noise. These are kisses of searching tongues. Only the air crushed between them dares express their desire: little mms, a gasp or two.

Even a hand on a belt is louder than their kiss.

The girl sees; a smile speaks volumes. Her stare says even more.

Really? Me?

Yes. You.

She couldn't find the words, but what is there to say? Heart pounds in ears; tongue sticks.

Her watch warns her,

"Tick. Tick."

The boy turns around. He and the girl reach for her like a silent film. Soon, she is wrapped in their embrace, somewhere between kissing both and neither, so far beyond saying hello or trading names.

Names mean nothing here.

Her body screams elation and consternation, delight and utter shame. The girl moves her against the books; her spine crushes smaller spines.

The kisses are harder now. Hands push harder, too.

Suddenly, she is not embraced, but devoured. The girl and boy maul her with sharp tongues. The girl's mouth sucks out all the air she so desperately needs. The boy handles her heart, draining her life, her dreams, that rent she has to pay, that panel at 2:45 she was so anxious to attend.

She is crushed, hardened, soon to be piled atop all else forgotten and untouched.

She tries to call for help, but no sound comes out.

BULLYING 101

—*an excerpt*

Iris was an excellent freak. It was her long-term extracurricular activity in lieu of soccer, lip gloss or gossip. If she had time to cultivate self-confidence she could have sneered down her oppressors, but tormentors followed from grade to grade, school to school, and by now it was far too late to reinvent her Self.

She dreamed of shoving off to the Big City, or anywhere big enough to get lost in. Oh the grace of anonymity! Where nobody knows your name…

She didn't have that. She had here, a town so stacked in prejudice she had her tortures down to a list.

THE HUMILIATION HANDBOOK

By: Iris McCarthy

Bullies are everywhere. Never fear! Once you can spot them on sight, you can avoid them. (Just kidding- they're everywhere.)

BULLY TYPES:

THE FAKE FRIEND- This bully will cajole, tease, humiliate etc., all in the name of "fun." Subsets: Gossipers, back-stabbers, two-facers and manipulators.

Worst of all: Web-Spinners. Avoid at all cost. They are the nicest to your face and the meanest behind your back.

Know them by their: fake smiles, fake nails, fake everything.

(Most of Iris' "friends" in junior high fell into this category, which is why she since abstained from socialization. She was only a child when she learned every relationship came with a price.)

THE REGULAR: This bully will torture you as a daily habit, like flossing. They will enlist 1-2 of the bullying tactics below, until you learn to avoid them by taking alternate routes, wearing bags over your head, attempting invisibility, etc.

Know them by their: beady eyes (perfect for spotting you at a distance.)

THE CRUSHER: The guy who's mean to you 'cause he wants to get in your pants but it's socially unacceptable to cavort with freaks.

Know them by their: blatant misogyny. (It smells like rotten eggs.)

THE JUDGE AND JURY: They stare at you, but don't worry: that's more than enough to make you feel like shit. They appear to scrutinize everything you are or do- your clothes, your walk, your existence. Best to close your eyes as soon as you smell one coming.

Know them by their: intense perfumes and/or frequent use of the Repulsion tactic (see below.)

THE JACKYL: Typical hanger-on for any of the above. They will laugh at anything stupid you do or anything any of the above parties say about you.

Know them by their: shrieking laughter which will ring in your ears for days.

THE HAUNTER: The Worst. This bully lives to see you die. Avoid at all cost, especially in very public places.*

*Including: hallways, cafeterias, gymnasiums, playgrounds, malls, auditoriums, concerts, parks, and anywhere else you might have fun.

Know them by their: hatred.

BULLY ARSENAL:

LOOKS:

THE SHAEDENFREUDER SNEER: Categorised by its ability to highlight faults you'd rather stay hidden. (Tripping in the hallway, answering a question wrong, or that damn zit right under your lip.)

SOLUTION #1: Be Perfect.

SOLUTION #2: Close your eyes.

THE LYNCH LOOK: Categorized by its ability to remind you that you never have and never will belong.

Note for racial minorities: this arsenal can be used with racist intent, or maybe you're just imagining that.

SOLUTION #1: Be Brave.
SOLUTION #2: Run away.

REPULSION RADAR: The Worst. A total distortion of the face, categorized by its ability to make you feel like a literal piece of shit. Do you smell? Are you really THAT ugly? Who knows, but whatever your problem is, you better fix it quick.

Often accompanied w/ dehumanizing pronouns (eg., "It.")

SOLUTION #1: AVOID AT ALL COSTS.

SOLUTION #2: Die?

(This ^ was this very look that inspired Iris to voluntary blindness.)

THE WORST WEAPON (AKA WORDS):

JABS- Appearance-based. (E.g., "Oh my god, can you believe it's wearing the ugliest skirt in the world?")

SOLUTION #1: Be Boring.

SOLUTION #2: Never wear that skirt again.

JIBES- Sexual-harassment: the early years. (E.g., "Why's she closing her eyes?" "She's waiting for me to cum on her face.")

SOLUTION #1: Uglify/do whatever you can to dissuade attention.

SOLUTION #2: Accept that you live in a patriarchy and will probably die in one too.

THREATS- Self-explanatory.

SOLUTION #1: Run!

SOLUTION #2: Keep running.

PSYCHIC SADISM- The Worst. I don't know how bullies can sense your deepest hurts, but they can. Bullies may in fact be empaths who decided to be dicks, which is disturbing on so many levels but um that's not the point here. (E.g., "Just kill yourself already!" "Freak." Etc. Etc. Etc.)

SOLUTION #1: Wear headphones everywhere, always.

SOLUTION #2: Don't wear headphones 'cause people will break or steal your discman four times before you finally give up.

Words-as-Weapons have various deployment systems:

THE TORPEDO SHOT- Often from a distance, loud enough to make you jump.

SOLUTION #1: Meditate daily to reset your nervous system.

SOLUTION #2: Move to Baffin Island. Your bullies would need a great diaphragm to reach you there.

THE SIDEWAY SNEER- Often in close quarters, never spoken TO you, but ABOUT you.

SOLUTION #1: Punch them in the face.

SOLUTION #2: Walk now. Cry later.

THE TIMELY SILENCE: How is it that girls are ALWAYS talking about you right before you enter a room?

SOLUTION #1: Punch them in the face.

SOLUTION #2: Avoid entering any room, ever.

THE IN-YOUR-FACE: Rare, but frightening. Reserved for angrier bullies on bad days. They will very deliberately invade your personal space, say something nasty, then walk away. It feels like rape.

SOLUTION #1: Close your eyes.

SOLUTION #2: Forgive them?

OTHER ARSENAL:

BRUISE-MAKING: Of little interest. If someone has to resort to fists, they are not very creative.

After this daily degradation, Iris hated teenagers. They were leeches with an acquired taste for tears.

Somewhere inside Iris was a big, beautiful woman who said, "Fuck It!" and lived like she wanted, who graffitied walls, set records, won awards, ate donuts, got tattooed and pierced and rolled in paint, who went to Paris, got married and divorced and married again, then stayed single for eternity, who boiled eggs, tamed tigers, sky-dived and base-jumped and played bass and fished bass and protested and punched and hugged and laughed and cried and tried and sometimes even won.

This girl and that life were waiting, but for now, Iris was in high school, and high school *sucked*.

B & E

The moon was not kissing the sky, but raping it.

Grounds: quiet, save for the chatter of rats nibbling at horses' hooves on rusted merry-go-rounds. Typewriters dusted, letters yawned on the floor. Stacks of badminton racquets, sacks of envelope wax, Magic-8 balls and rotary phones completed the inventory.

This was a warehouse of the unwanted. A haunted house of rejects. A graveyard for carnivals. A prison for memories.

Population: one: a security guard, underpaid, underslept, overjoyed to be alone. His boots scraped forgotten floors, and he struggled to imagine these bits and baubles bringing joy to parents now dead and children now grown, suffocated by certainties such as taxes and death.

All was dust coating old worlds like a seal.

A clink! superseded by a clatter. Baton at the ready! The guard's flashlight flickered in private excitement before landing on a figure at the end of the cramped, cluttered space.

A B&E, here?

Why would anyone want to break in here?

The stranger stumbled, hands raised as if in praise. The guard was soon upon him, close enough to see bits of blood on wrist and chin.

Then he understood.

"Now then, where did you come from?"

This sorry sod was in no shape to fight, and could only surrender to the devious impulse of telling the truth.

"Over there." a raised hand cast a sad shadow. "The arcade."

Here he thought it was going to be a quiet night. A virginal notebook slipped from the guard's pocket, and held his first notes of disapproval.

The offender creaked forward. His knuckles curled all the way in, as if he hadn't moved in ages. Or maybe he'd spent the whole time making fists.

The guard had to ask,

"How did you do it?"

Their eyes met, dangerously close to knowing each other. The intruder was the first to shatter any potential intimacy.

"It wasn't what I expected."

"It never is." the guard looped their arms, and courted the delinquent past stuffed bears with no stuffing, books in want of readers, forks in need of plates, popcorn machines long obsolete.

The guard was surprised when the intruder entered a soliloquy.

"Get an idea in your head, act on it. It's a lark, really. Until you get caught."

An employed man knows better than to partake in too much philosophy. Instead he replied,

"Let's see what damage you did."

The best weapon was poised between his fingers: a pen. He noted the time, the place, the who's. As for Why's or How's, he only had blank space.

From the way the stranger walked, one might think he knew the place.

They arrived. The security guard inspected the entrance, the door whose hinges were wrenched, the knob furiously tampered with.

"Did you do that?"

A nod from his weary companion. The guard shook his head.

"That's going to have to be fixed."

Another nod from the man, iconoclast turned to sycophant.

The mighty pen transcribed while a guard's boot nudged the door in case it might fall on their heads. It proved its efficacy, and in they went.

The ceiling was all windows, and for a moment the suspense was suspended by that voracious moon, the poetry of those perfect clouds, the solace of the proud stars.

Their attention turned to rows and rows of pinball machines. Some were too old for the guard to recognize, while others were reminiscent of his childhood. Again he witnessed old, dead innocence crushed under time.

Halfway down the first row was a conspicuously open space. The machine astride this vacancy boasted shattered glass. Winking shards fraternized with bumper coils sans chaperone.

"You do that too?"

After a shrug, the intruder was compelled to elaborate.

"It was dark. Landed right on it. Couldn't be helped."

This time, a sigh punctuated the notebook's scribbles.

"That's going to have to be fixed too!"

The man awaited punishment.

"Are you going to get back-up?"

"No," the guard looked confused with pity, "I can deal with you myself."

He raised his baton just high enough.

"Sit down. Please."

The criminal wedged himself in the empty area, careful to avoid the glass.

Cursing his own empathy, the guard raised his baton one more time.

"I am sorry."

The B&E tried to smile.

"Can't be helped. At least I tried. Right?"

The stick met its mark.

Job done, the guard retreated from the room, Case #1 duly recorded in his now trusty notebook.

He left all the pinball machines in their proper place.

Not a space between them was missing.

CHASING BILL

It's shit being a med student mannequin.

Fashion dolls have it easy: brand names and window views!

I got a tough gig. You wouldn't believe what we have to put up with, especially concerning the sadistic fuckers, of which there are many.

I won't get into that. All you need to know is I'm a teaching mannequin at the Big City University in the clinical simulation centre, Room 9-37-C, and a virus is going to be released into the building.

My name's Bill.

Nice to meet you.

***

You'd be amazed what people say when they think no one's listening.

Unfortunately for them, someone always is.

I would have felt sorry for him if he'd been a loser. If the girls didn't date him, if the boys ignored or worse, bullied him, but it's not like that. Chase is a basic bitch. Decent-looking. Average grades. He would float by if he was born free of the mad streak that makes destruction more appealing than creation.

You see it when he looks at a girl. It's even worse when he looks at us mannequins. It's a look that says, "You're mine to do whatever I want with."

He always stayed overnight in the lab; I know because you can't get to it without walking through the CSC and they always leave me lying around. One night, he left late, and sat by me to light up a cigarette.

"It's soon." he said- to himself, not to me, though his eyes bore deep into mine. God, I wished I could blink.

"Soon they'll all pay."

Pay for what? As far as I could see, he was dealt a decent hand. Certainly better than me! All he could do was plot carnage because he lacked the imagination to do anything better.

I have no idea what kind of virus it is. Knowing him, it'll be airborne, lethal, and painful. And traceable, because he doesn't care about escape. All he wants is to drag as many people into his Hell as he can.
If only I could run into the lab and smash his precious work. Dial for police. Leave a note on someone's desk.

This body is useless.

There's only one thing I can do.

***

I practice with sleepers.

They're easier.

I feel bad. These kids work so long and so hard. They're innocent, and I must exploit their vulnerability. For their own sake.

I practice every day, and every night I see Chase leave the lab I want to wave and smirk but all I can do is think,
Just you wait.

***

Today's the day. He's nervous, and stops for an early cigarette.

Perfect.

I pull, pull, pull, DRAG him in. He feels nothing, at first, then his arm jerks, but by the time he screams, it's too late.

He doesn't deserve that body; I do.

AHHHHHHHHHHHHHHH WTF WTF

Oh… um…

WHERE AM I? WHY CAN'T I MOVE? WHO ARE YOU? WHAT THE FUCK WHAT THE FUCK WHAT THE

Um… I appear to have made a mistake. You see, I intended to switch bodies with you.

WHAT THE FUCK WHAT THE FUCK WHAT

Looks like we're both trapped in my body instead.

BUT. I CAN'T MOVE. I'M NOT BREATHING. WHAT KIND OF BODY IS THIS?

It's, um, a med student mannequin? Like the ones you used to throat-fuck for fun. Remember that?

GET ME OUT OF HERE YOU FUCKING FREAK. I HAVE SHIT TO DO.

Not anymore! Ah well. This wasn't exactly how I planned it, but at least you won't be releasing that virus!

YOU FUCKING FREAK YOU FUCKING FREAK YOU

My name's Bill.
Nice to meet you!

PARTING GIFT (BEFORE WE SAY GOODBYE)

Nothing inside you will ever be small.

Many things -sometimes too many- will erupt in your heart and mind. This will result in itches, diarrhea, self-doubt.

Anger will be hard to control, even more difficult to express.

Sometimes the world will burst within you, and as much as you try to claw it out, scare it off, mosh it free, it will remain.

Descending from the outer realm, you will never be able to quiet down. Your dial is forever turned up to 11. Most humans are set at 3.

Take, for example, next Friday.

You will wake up at 6:35 AM. The sheets will be heavy, having made you sweat all night, and your dreams, which always seem so important when you're having them, will ebb. Your shoulder blade will spasm; your ears will explode like a bomb went off and you'll stare at the ceiling in wonder until you shoot piss in the toilet bowl followed by other items best left to euphemism.

You will wipe, flush, wash your hands, brush your teeth for less time than you should.

At 7:35 AM you will die/resurrect yourself in the shower.

At 10:38 you will walk to the library because you're dying to get your hands on Virginia Woolf, and besides, you need to return Michelle Tea.

You, like all humans, will be clueless as to what is going to happen, which is why I'm attempting to enlighten you.

A mood swing will hit before you reach the door. You will detour to a small tree. The Madness will impale for a moment, and that moment will feel like forever, but if you remember your DBT techniques, you will enter the library sane.

No angel will come down to help you. Forever you are severed from home.

The best thing you can do is stop looking for rescue. Stop viewing yourself as a victim. Stop worrying what's going to happen next.

The gate is closing. This is the last you'll hear from me. All I can say is you are destined to lose it, but will find it again.
And, whatever you do, do not walk around to the back of the building. Do not remain at that tree too long.

Dry your tears. Walk inside.

As fast as you possibly can.

BEAUTY VS BEAST

I need a break.

The club's dead in January. Bills that would otherwise line our ankle purses are allocated for kids, wives, mistresses. When New Year's rolls around, belts are tight, wallets tighter.

Besides, *that thing* happened in November.

I never thought it would happen.

I never expected to do what I did.

In want of an overpriced getaway, I log on to that overpriced getaway site.

Where are you going?

Anywhere!

Check In

Right the fuck now.

Check Out

Never?

Guests

Just me. Like always.

I tell the search engine I'm "flexible" (less true now than at twenty-two), and peruse Cabins.

I want somewhere I can be someone else. Maybe even be myself.

Cozy A-Frame with Sleek Modern Interior

Ooh. Click!

Our home is perfectly situated for all your adventures!

Stunning loft

Modern appliances

Maintaining a classic, cozy feel.

Complete with twinkle lights!

$449/night.

Worth it.

***

Self check-in is great when the keypad works.

6-6-6

I'm in…!

I've been catfished!

The cabin abused filters, aerial angles and an inviting nighttime ambience to reel me in! Irl, it's a triangular sylvan stack on a teetering butte with a bumpy parking spot and one of those annoying ovens that beeps too loud.

Worst of all, the twinkle lights are MIA.

At least there's a lake view.

The guest book corroborates:

"Amazing view!'
"Great lake!"

Ad nauseam, ad infinitum.

I almost puke.

I tiptoe across the silence.

Didn't Edith Wharton write about how loud quiet can be?

Stunning emptiness. I'm in a black hole made of oak.

Is this what people want when they "get away"?

Maybe silence feels different when there's someone to share it with.

Couples have demeaned these couches, counters, the first and second queen beds. This place is a tribute to the desperate fuck.

No matter where I go, work follows.

I stock the fridge with (my) essentials: wheatgrass juice, overnight oats, CBD oil.

My yoga mat unravels for some bad bitch poses but I opt instead to stroke spines of books no one reads.

I think of The Beast, as he's dubbed in all the parlours and clubs. You'd think I'd heed the warnings of other dancers (i.e., "Watch out for him.") but they tend to be prejudicial bitches (e.g., "Brown guys are cheap.")

I trust the universe, and customers by proxy.

There's never a problem.

Until there is.

***

The Beast haunts me.

I read, stretch, walk nowhere (great idea, renting a cabin in January.)

I'm stuck in my head with him.

My fifth reading attempt is doomed to be DNF'd in the loft on a stodgy mattress under red and white wallpaper. Who decided to dress up a lodge like a peppermint stick? It's enigmatic in all its ugliness. I intensify my gaze of the unbecoming stripes, hoping to uncover the meaning of life beneath. If I can't figure out life in general, solving my own would be nice.

The sun is cold and white, perfect for highlighting stretch marks and cellulite. It's even worse for the wall. Every kiss, slip, bump and handprint is made visible as a viscid, shiny streak.

Bathed in sunlight, I see what shouldn't be seen.

Handprints. Scratches. Swirls. It suggests a language born of evil intelligence.

All symbols converge into a paralyzing pentagram.

Fucking great. The cabin lacks twinkle lights, but comes with a built-in ouija board?

I rest my hand on a stranger's print. One touch and my body is juiced.

I see their terrified faces. I hear their terrible screams.

I'm manic, panicked, terrified. This cabin hosts parades of paranoia, breakdowns and battlegrounds.

Bad things happen in this house.

The guest book deserves further investigation. I angle it into the light, and hate what I find.

There's that same sticky shimmer underneath what is easily seen.

"Amazing view (of the hell dimension!)"

"Great lake (to drown yourself in!)"

Ad infinitum, ad nauseam.
This time, I vomit for real.

Fight or flight manifests differently in everyone. The coward (i.e. survivor) in me wants to GTFO ASAP. My inner fighter (ie fool) is game for an exorcism. I bet they have tutorials on Youtube! I could chant, read tomes, smoke out this place…

It's one thing to think a fear.

It's another to feel it.

There's something here.

The atmosphere thickens. Oxygen becomes electric. The more I breathe, the less air I get. My terror is palpable enough to push walls.

I wipe my mouth of its swill, too scared to turn on the faucet, let alone wash my hands. Every move is scrutinized.

I've been watched this whole time.

I thought there was nothing worse than loneliness, but that's not true.

The worst thing is being alone with someone you don't want to be alone with.

I'm halfway down the loft's stairs when I hear it behind me.

I don't want to see, but ignorance is worse.

It's seven feet tall: head scrapes ceiling. Mangy musk conjures up a possessed puppet from a church's nursery: matted, brown hair glued onto an abominable sock. It only has two teeth, but that's enough: one sits at the middle top of its gaping, red mouth, while one resides at the bottom, curled the wrong way, impacting infectious gums.

It's The Beast.

Men like him are monsters in disguise.

When he entered the club (in human form), girls scattered like moths. He looked like a bowling ball with legs, like anyone else who sees strippers on a Thursday.

Why would I refuse him a dance? We don't get an hourly fucking wage. Our income relies on our charm, our ability to listen and laugh. We don't sell sex. We provide connection.

Only the rarest want something more: something that isn't theirs, and never will be.

Nearing the song's end, I had yet to remove my panties. His big belly made for a little lap, and I struggled to bounce intimacy off his leaden eyes.

He grabbed me, flipped me over, held me down, and shoved a finger inside.

He raped me with his hand, put me down and left.

What did I do?

Nothing.

What could I have done? Cause a scene, make a fuss? Why? He paid me the twenty upfront. I faced down The Beast, like every Beauty must. Next time I'll avoid him, maybe warn the new kid to look out.

The human mind is powerful. What you focus on is what you create. When imagination is amplified by a bedevilled space, watch out.

Most of us have no idea what we're wishing for.

I did want this.

I wanted the chance to make it right.

"So, you followed me? I reckon you ain't here for the view."

He rarely spoke in human form; I don't expect eloquent expostulations now.

His jowls ooze hungry fluids. He's had a taste of my fear, and wants more. He feeds on it. He'll devour me inside out.

I retreat backwards down the steps, tiptoeing across the screaming silence. It's only my breath and his, louder than a thunderstorm on fire.

No matter where I go, he'll track me down. My fear leaves a perfume.

I only have one weapon, and I will wield it well.

"LOVE." I cry.

The Beast slows its descent. Encouraged, I elaborate.

"LOVE IS BETTER THAN YOU. LOVE IS STRONGER. LOVE IS LOUDER. LOVE. LOVE. LOVE…!"

I scream the most magical word in the world until it fills the room, fights the fear and wins.

Love is all I have to give or keep.
He can never take it away from me.

Love can't kill monsters, but it does disorient them. He falters long enough for my escape. I ditch all my worldly bullshit except wallet and keys.

Fuck this horror haven! It doesn't even have twinkle lights!

I slip on the crackling snow in bare feet. I run like Roger Bannister, like Tyler Durden, like Forest fucking Gump.

I literally run for my life.

I've run like this before: from crazy roommates, drunk lovers. I'll run as long as it takes.

To hell with holidays.

I can't wait to get back to work.

GHOSTS EVERYWHERE

I can still feel your fingers on my nipples.

I can still hear your laugh in my ear.

All I've got is the ghost.

At least I was able to sleep in 'cause my new custodial job at Colonial Park doesn't start until 2PM, because apparently nobody litters in an "outdoor living history museum" before noon.

Turns out rock bottom is a garbage can- one you are responsible for emptying.

***

On the bus, everyone's staring at their phones to avoid eye contact. I wonder when the bosses of the world will fix that. Seems all they care about is going to space.

The bus drops me off on an ominous loop, Colonial Park 15 minutes away. I endure (and sometimes enjoy) the stares from cars as I walk in my tight black slacks and tight blue tank.

I was promised a t-shirt in my interview, and from the sun's glare, I'm going to need it.

I find Administration. Boss #1 tells me to go sit with the other cleaners:

two Black guys, two white guys (one who shows up late), one Ambiguous Ethnic Guy and a Brown Girl, the latter of whom is also on their first day.

White Guy #1 talks with Boss #1 about some other guy who by all accounts should be in for work, but isn't.

Then we walk.

There's a big sign behind the train station that says:

DRINK WATER. DON'T DIE.

We enter the early 20th century before I've signed on. I have, however, sweat through my shirt so much it's an entirely different shade of blue. My colleagues walk slow, presumably to preserve energy.

There are only a few actors out. I admire their silly bonnets and lace fringe. There's a handsome white boy with "brown paper packages tied up with strings", a pretty Black girl who fans herself on a patio. There's a huge white lady in a giant sun hat and a white man with a bowler hat, bottleneck glasses and blonde Charlie Chaplin moustache. Everyone says, "Good day", and only ever come out of character when they talk to us, the help.

The Staff Room is on the second floor of the druggist. I always longed to pass behind those ropes marked Staff Only. The stairs creak, we sign in, and I ask Boss #2 for my t-shirt.

"Yeahhh. I'll have to ask them for more." she stares at her phone for protection.

Guess I'm wearing this: my sweat-soaked, low-cut tank top in the screaming sun, working with mostly teenage boys.

Good thing I brought sunscreen.

Colonial Park is divided into eras: 1920, 1905, 1880-something, and, of course, the Fort, which boasts an 18th century air. (Not that I'm an expert.)

Everything feels romantic until I lug my first garbage bag into its disposable compartment.

From 2-5PM, it's chill. Mostly walking (in the blazing hot sun, in a shirt that's begging me to get skin cancer) the route of garbage cans and washrooms across the park. I will have mapped this place solely by its garbage cans and washrooms.

My shoulders crackle with the sun.

When the park closes at 5, the real work starts. We sweep, mop, scrub. Some buildings don't have their own cleaning supplies, so we lug wet mops over blocks and blocks of wooden platform.

Plus, lucky us, someone vomited on the boardwalk!

I don't know how I fucked up this badly- at life, or at love. I don't know how the one Tinder guy I decided to date turned out to have anger issues. I don't know how I can be almost thirty with a bank account that waffles between $-45 and $13, and a perpetual Visa bill paid off every month by my parents.

You have to start wherever you are.

I'm here, eyeing a toilet that smells like it was preserved from the 1880s.

Fun fact: we do not disinfect the toilets.

I am instructed, instead, to wet a paper towel, and wipe the rim.

I'm never peeing in public again.

***

Second day. I got up in time to work out but my ass ached so I opted out.

Maybe today they'll give me a t-shirt.

Maybe tomorrow my life will get back together.

It doesn't work that way. Success and failure are slow processes. Our choices both indicate and direct the trajectory of our self-development.

I hope this choice makes me a better person. In the long run, at least.

Breaking up with you was the right thing. Even the honeymoon phase went to shit. You kept saying you wanted to make love but we only fucked. And you couldn't even remain calm for my birthday weekend, even though I told you my deepest, darkest secret about why I hate my birthday so much.

One thing I'm noticing: everyone here is a slacker, except White Boy #1. He has to force White Boy #2 and Black Boy #1 to do anything at all (and we usually redo their work.)

Eg. Masonic Hall. WB1 and I cleaned three different buildings on 1905 St while WB2 and BB1 lazed their way through the restaurant. Their mopping was so bad we had to redo it for them, after which BB1 pointed out the mop bucket and told us to dump it.

"Why don't you?" I said, in my cheeriest tone.

He obliged, much to my pleasure.

The others are worse. I've yet to work with Black Boy #2 but apparently he "gets lost" ie ditches for his shift, always wandering back in time for breaks. The Brown Chick left work two hours early on her first day, and Ambiguous Ethnic Boy is sweet, but a little too sweet to be a hard worker. White Boy #1 is manning this ship by the skin of his teeth, and me, I'm mixing metaphors.

On break, Ambiguous Ethnic Boy offers to take me for coffee.

I'd rather be alone.

Or as alone as I can be in the break room.

I remember coming here as a kid. I was fascinated by the fur pelts, gift shop arrowheads, root beer candy sticks. The guides never mentioned genocide. They made it sound like the whites and Natives were friends.

Maybe my problem is always wanting to see the good in people. Wanting to see people at all.

I want to feel wanted, like I have a purpose, a reason for being. Apart from picking up garbage.

Somebody has to do it.

Never thought that someone would be me.
Privilege will bite you in the ass eventually.

Anytime I see some guy with dark eyebrows and blue eyes, my heart bends the wrong way. Thankfully there's a deficit of sexy buff dudes roaming Colonial Park on a Thursday. There's mostly families of four, and, to my surprise, hipster couples, perhaps attending ironically.

I lean out the window of the Drugstore/Staff Room. This building might have memories, but it's probably a reconstruction.

I watch one of the impersonators walk the grass past the horses. He's the one in the bowler hat. As tall as you, but skinnier, and looking about as sad as me.

He walks towards the 1920s until he disappears.

Literally.

***

It's weird to work somewhere haunted. Your coworkers accept paranormal phenomenon as a given, rather than a subject of intrigue or debate.

I told White Boy #1 about my ghost and they went, "Oh, sure, yeah."

Seriously? We're cavorting with beings from the beyond, and it's just another Thursday?

So what if it happens all the time. Shouldn't that make us care more?

What happened to wonder? I will always remember how it felt to watch a human figure fizzle out of existence. It made me remember how delicate it all is.

Any moment, I could fizzle too.

***

TGIF- except I work weekends.

Not counting tax deductions, I'll have made 371.25 by the end of today. It almost makes me want to stay.

Money may not buy happiness, but maybe it can buy self-esteem. Of which I am in desperate need, living at my parents' place sleeping on a saggy mattress because they didn't get an Extra Firm one like I asked.

There's no time to think about you. Too many life areas are in desperate need of reconstruction- or demolition. Maybe you can't have one without the other.

Anyway, I'm obsessed with this ghost.

I've done some digging:

There are several "hot spots" in Colonial Park, especially the Henberg House (moved from its original spot in 1976.) People report footsteps, flickering lights, the smell of tobacco. Actual sightings are few.

I'll bet that's where my guy was headed.

WB1 tells me to get my head out of the clouds and back to the garbage.

"If you go looking for ghosts, you'll never find any."

I don't care. The ghost showed itself. They wanted to be seen. I understand them, which means they may understand me.

***

I'm on a steady diet of chocolate and self-loathing. I have Jenny Slate and Hannah Gadsby on repeat 'cause they're the only comedians I find funny, ie not triggering.

I keep sleeping in. When I come home from work I scroll through Ghost Hunter videos until it dawns on me those Anti-Phone people may have a point.

Then I scroll some more.

When I broke up with you, you said (well, messaged):

"Remember: don't let anyone treat you as less than you deserve."
"I know. That's why I'm ending this."- that's what I wanted to reply.

There's been too many guys like you. Every time I meet a new one I think I've broken the pattern, only to find you're the same ghoul in different skin. The only difference this time: I ended it, and quick.

But it was already too late.

You're in my heart- or is it my head? Your baby voice talking to your cat. Your scent (bourbon, pheromones, Dolce and Gabbana cologne, cigarettes.) Your weird-ass taste in music (doo-wop, Americana, good country and bad rap.)

Thirteen hours into our breakup I convinced myself I was overreacting. Then I remembered when I cried on your balcony on my birthday eve thinking, "What the fuck is up with him?" or how I started to fret whether or not that or this would make you mad.

"I'm sorry I'm not perfect"- another of your messages.

I don't want perfection. I just want you to handle your shit.

You have insomnia, and guzzle caffeine. You get hangry, and never eat. You have a Standard, Commercial, and Class M driver's license, and you get road rage!

You are your own worst enemy. And I'm too weak to stand up to your bullshit. I am human tofu; I collect the flavour of whatever I'm with.

For now I will mate with guitars, eat extra chocolate and cry. I cry when I work out; I cry on the bus headed downtown because I want to walk by your building and see you wave from the balcony but that's all over, and damn was it over fast.

I should get bubble tea with a friend. Invest in more sunscreen. Enjoy my free trial of Spotify Premium.

Set goals. Meet them.

Instead I'm hunting ghosts.

***

You've deleted me from Facebook.

My message about whether or not you want your Vitamin E lotion back went ignored for too long, so I clicked on your profile.
FB mocked me with:
Do you know Scott?

Of course I know you! You've been inside of me!
Now, what am I? Nothing?
Am I even worth a memory?

I broke up with you. I know that. But that doesn't mean I want our entire world erased. Facebook is my only way of finding you, ever knowing you're okay. You have one public status about a new job, and that's it. I don't know what the job is. It could be smuggling cocoa leaf, vintage tea pots, or children. You might have gone into wrestling, or finally joined the police academy.

I walk through work in a daze. White Boys 1 and 2 argue about which pizza is best.

I lose it with Black Guy #2 when he claims his paper towel isn't good enough to wipe the walls, and makes at going to find something else.

"Here. You can have my cloth." I hand it to him.

"Oh, it's not wet enough! I'll go…"

"NO." I snap. "It's fine. Get to it."

He obliges; I am vindicated. Ambiguous Ethnic Guy gives me a thumbs up.

Another day, another $115.

We've finished with enough time for me to find the haunted house.

It's locked. I can only peer through the windows and will my bloodless buddy appear.

They say you never find something while you're looking, but that's just not true.

The best things are only found when you hunt them down.

His face appears in the second floor window. He puffs his pipe and stares.

Then he mouths words which are unmistakable:

"Fuck off."

***

At least it's beautiful here.

There are chickens, pigs. One time I sang to the cow.

I research apparitions every break. Ample ghost hunters have "investigated" the Henberg House, usually with an Echo Vox, which I deem bullshit.

I find a clip where a voice says:
"Just leave."

That's my guy for sure.

***

I'm getting tan, and fit. I'm too tired to eat when I get home, too hot to even nibble my sandwich. I subsist on morning eggs and a Larabar in the afternoon. The Janitor's Diet! Soon it'll be trending.

White Boy #1 and I work the ice cream parlour. The vendors mop at the end of their shift, but WB1 tells me to do it again because they leave streaks.

My shoulders used to ache from this; now they guide the mop with ease.

I glance up the street. Cars sometimes roll by: stock delivery, security, all which ruin the effect of the closed Park.

Then I see him, bowler hat shirking the sunset.

"Shit." WB1 says to the garbage cans. "This one's out of compost bags."
"I'll get some!"

I bolt to the ghost, who, when he sees me, books it.

He stays solid until we hit the greenhouse, then he's nothing but air.

"Wait! I want to talk to you! Please!"

I hear him sigh.

"I don't want to talk. I just want to be left alone."

"Seriously? But, ghosts are supposed to have unfinished business. I figured you'd want someone to…"

"Well, I'm sorry I don't satisfy your stereotypical expectations."

"But…"

"Just leave."

He's gone.

***

I fall in love too easily.

You warned me:
"Don't equate sex with love."

I can't help it. I'm too sensitive- physically and emotionally. I get too attached, and I cling too hard.

I thought it would be different because I was the one who ended it. But it's even worse.

While WB1 and I sweep the fire station, BB1 and WB2 stare until WB1 has to literally yell at them to go work.

Despite this, we finish early again. They play pool in the saloon while I watch the horses graze. Brown Girl and Black Boy #2 have disappeared, leaving Ambiguous Ethnic Boy stuck checking garbages.

The incompetence in this workplace is startling. I know we only get minimum wage, but isn't that worth something? We get to walk around a gorgeous park all day, surrounded by nature and history.

Maybe they don't appreciate it like I do. Black Boy #1 even said once,

"I can't believe these stupid bitches actually pay to walk around here."

WB1 exits the saloon, and invites me to play.

"Want to fill in? White Boy #2 isn't playing anymore."

What's this? An invitation to normalcy?

They're playing snookers. I relax when I see WB1 is as bad a player as me.

I'm stuck with an awful shot, the cueball out of my reach.

"Just get up on the table!" suggest the boys.

"This isn't a music video!"
They laugh- and blush.

I'm still attractive. I still know how to have fun. My life isn't over. My heart will go bloody on.

Then I see Bosses 1 and 2 at the door.

"Hi!" I wave.

Something in their body language stops my hand halfway.

***

"You need to be working!"

All the work was done.

"You cannot go anywhere customers can see you!"
The Park was closed.

"Playing pool? Having fun? No!"

We're not allowed to have fun?

Of course not. We're the help. We can't be touching anything but toilets with wet paper towel. We daren't relax, or blow off steam.

We aren't worthy.

Boss #1 pulls White Boy #1 out of the room, leaving Boss #2 to hawk-eye the rest of us.

Meanwhile, White Boy #2 is eager to throw his friend under the bus.

"I told WB1 he shouldn't do that."

I stare daggers. No one wants a rat, especially in a cleaning job. How convenient that he left the pool hall right before the managers came.

89

White Boy #1 is the most competent worker they have! Everyone else either disappears or half-asses. They should be the ones in trouble, not him!

I'm the type of girl who stays quiet. Most of the time I say yes, and if I can't do that, I smile.

We can only start where we are, and I'm here, with the chance to stick up for a friend.

"I'd like to vouch for White Boy #1. I haven't been here long, but he has been so helpful. I honestly can't imagine what this job would be like without him."

My impassioned speech makes little difference- certainly not for the better. White Boy #1 and and Boss #2 are back, and we all know he's fired.

"Oh?" Boss #1 is in a mood for a challenge. "Would you like to leave with him?"

I force my soaked, sore body to stand.

"Whatever. I'm done here."

***

Ambiguous Ethnic Boy, whose name is Baqir, walks me out.

"That was wrong, what they did. They shouldn't have fired him. And they shouldn't have fired you. It was good of you to defend him, Karen."

I cringe at my name. Baqir notices.

"You don't like your name?"
"Hate it. I've always wanted to change it."

"To what?"

"Not sure yet."

"What are you going to do for work?"
I laugh.

"Not sure yet?"

"That's okay." Baqir picks up garbage on the way; he's a better worker than I thought. "You'll figure it out. You're smart, and, you know, well, you're pretty."

He walks me to the bus stop.

"Good luck, Karen! Let me know when you change your name!"

He rolls his bike away.

I won't fall in love with this one. I need to focus on myself. I need to move out, get a job, get over you, figure out what it means to be human.

I'll make more mistakes. I'll collect more ghosts, waste more days.

I'll get better at letting go.

The bus is late. I wait and wait and wait and then I see the dead guy in a bowler hat walk towards me.

He mimics sitting on the bench, but the wood goes through his knees.

"Heading off, are we?" he smokes his pipe.

"I thought you wanted to be left alone."

He shrugs, smoke spirals rolling into the red sun.

"What I hope for you, my dear, is that you remain a good person. From what I can tell, there aren't many left."

He looks younger than me, but I know better than to judge appearances. This is a wise, ancient man.

His lips puff around his pipe.

"Most people, when they see me, are afraid. They run the other way. You ran towards me. Perhaps I rejected your company because it was so unexpected."
"Sometimes we push people away." I say it to him, but I think of you.

"Little bird told me you want to change your name." Puff-puff. "I did, you know. When I came here."

"Really?"

He puts a faint finger to his lips.

"That's a secret between you and me. What name are you considering?"

"Um, I don't know? But I do like the name Eden. I know it's not practical or anything but…"

"Paradisiacal! It suits you."

My clothes are glued to my skin. I'll be lucky if I can saw my hair out of this ponytail.

"Really?"

"You are worth more than you think."

When my ride arrives I'm alone, crying the happiest tears.

HELP US

A boyfriend and girlfriend walk down the street like they're the only people who matter, and why not?

Love makes the whole world smaller.

He sneaks a grab at her ass. Why not? They are young, it's 16 above, and most folks are inside under quarantine. (Exempting the mother-son-father triad across the street, mother and father turned into trapeze with the cry, "Un, deux, trois!" On "trois!" they swing their son by his hands to grant him a glimpse of infinity. "That's my favourite," he says. Mom thinks he means the park, but I know he means that game of mocking gravity, that joyous burst of living few forget.)

(Oh. And me. I'm two feet behind the boyfriend-girlfriend, on the sunny side of the street.)

I hold a wallet in one hand, and The Fellowship of the Ring in the other- though I doubt I'll have time to read.

In other news, face masks have become an accessory. They are the #1 Bestseller on Etsy, and have been so for four weeks. Capitalism is nothing if not opportunistic.

Same goes for young lovers. He tries her ass again. I begin to wonder if they are not so much lovers as lusters. And why not? They are young. Younger than me, and probably younger than you.

They curve towards the park. I track them with what I hope is subtlety. They don't see me, and they are all who matter. They are the only kids in the world who needn't worry.

Their refuge is under a tree. The boy takes out his phone, the girl asks about his feelings, the boy responds as if his feelings belong to someone else, and they might.

It is a gorgeous day. We've been waiting so long for Spring, and now that it's here, none of us are allowed to enjoy it.

The boyfriend-girlfriend should not be outside. Lucky for them, the police rarely enforce quarantine downtown. Too much hassle hassling the poor. Too much risk hassling the rich. Best to advise precautions and leave it be.

Most of us are all too happy to obey.

Neither the boy or the girl are sick, and they never will be.

Not if I have anything to say about it.

My heart is at a thousand bpm. I wish I could make this impersonal, but can't. They matter as much as me. I am just as human as them.

Crisis forces the most unimportant people into the big picture.

I slide the needle into their necks- first her, then him. They slip into what appears to be a pleasant sleep, as my superior promised.

I must convince myself they are not in pain, and pray they never need feel pain again. Should the necessary experiments cause discomfort or -perish the thought- agony, I can only rest in the assurance that it is all for the greater good.

The pickup is quick. Two stretchers, four men, a nondescript van.

We do not talk. We don't need to. Nor do we touch. We can't.

If I have done my job right -and I'm certain I have- we have bagged and tagged the only two souls in the Big City with confirmed immunity. If we can isolate, extract and replicate their defences, these young lovers will be more famous for their sacrifice than Romeo and Juliet, and for a far nobler cause.

The men treat them as cargo, but I memorize their faces, free of masks, as if unconsciously aware of their in-borne resilience. How lovely it must be.

How lovely it must have been.

I savour one final glance before the bags are zipped, stretchers shipped to the right people at the right place and right time to save the world and make history.

J R R Tolkein said, "only a small part is played in great deeds by any hero." He also said, "Nothing is evil in the beginning", and I can't be sure that's true. A virus this terrible must have been birthed by evil, and any attempt to cure it must be tinged with evil too.

COBWEBS

She used to watch spiders dance, make skirts out of their webs, and clap for each other at parties.

Their pinchers would click with arachnid laughter at arachnid jokes she couldn't understand.

Then those nasty pills came, and tried to stomp out all the spiders.

Sometimes she could still hear them click. One or two would tip-toe across empty dance floors, reminiscent of good times long past.

Then the pills would stomp in with their big, ugly boots, full of nasty dyes and suspicious substances. They would boom, boom, boom, and stomp, stomp, stomp, and all the spiders would scatter.

Why did everyone hate the spiders? They were nice to her. They played with her when no one else would.

The men with white gloves said the spiders were a symptom of her sickness. They sat her on couches, strapped her on beds, fed her Monte Cristo sandwiches and lentil loaf because she was vegetarian. And pills. Always pills. Blue, pink, yellow, purple, red, creating a rainbow tummy ache.

The spiders ran scarce. They were scared. They whispered warnings to their brethren of the doctors, the nurses, the meds.

She begged them to stay, but they were too afraid.

All except one.

This spider was a good hider. She hid in the toolbox of the girl's brain whenever the pills came. Their flashlights would almost catch the tips of her scruffy hair, but God and guile saved her. She scuffled through the empty cabinets that had once been full. Much had been cleared out by the pills: anything deemed suspicious or superfluous.

One night, the spider slipped past the armed guards and onto the girl's hair.

"Psst!"

The girl and the spider saw each other. For the first time between those barren, white walls, the patient smiled.

"I thought you'd all gone!"

"Everyone but me!"

The spider danced on her fingers, and kissed each one. She giggled; her fingers tickled.

"Will you stay?"

"Always."

The spider hopped back inside her brain before the nurse made her hourly check.

The hospital was nicer after that. No matter her brain's bonfires, the spider would escape unscathed. They shared chocolate pudding; the spider taught her the delicate art of webspinning.

When we get comfortable, we make mistakes. The girl admitted to a doctor that one spider still visited. It was concluded the pills needed reinforcements.

The girl warned her friend the night before her treatment,

"You have to hide! The lightning will fry you for sure."

How could she bear to leave her dear girl all alone? Despite her better instincts, the spider obeyed, and watched while they dragged her sedated friend away.

Once upon a time, a little girl saw people's auras. She made friends with spiders. She remembered people's names.

All of that went away.

The girl missed eating cherries and running through the rain, but she couldn't leave until she was better, and she wouldn't be better until she told the spider to go away.

They agreed: lying was the was the only way to escape. So she told the doctors all the spiders had left. No, she didn't hear them dance. No, she never saw them use webs as parachutes.

Yes, she would like to go home.

The doctors loved her lies. The more she lied, the happier they became, and soon they made arrangements to set her free outside these dank, white walls into a very real world.

One doctor was disappointed. He had been especially interested in her case. Unlike the newer doctors -so insipid, so naive!- he maintained all mental illness was degenerative, with only one sure cure.

He promised the parents that, though experimental, his techniques were the most effective. They consented that their daughter participate. They wanted her happy, healthy, and home.

The spider overheard when she was munching flies, and warned her friend.

"I heard the doctor. He wants to keep some of your brain."

"What can we do?" she fretted.

"We have to escape!"

"How? They still restrain me at night. The doors need swipe cards. There's night nurses, and security guards. And there's too many people around during the day."

"They're going to do it to you tomorrow morning! We have to do something!"

The girl looked out the window, glass so thick it sometimes blurred the trees.

"This place will never let go of me. They'll always keep the best parts for themselves. You know I don't even dream anymore? How much worse will it be after they cut me open?"

When the girl smiled, it only made the spider worry more.

"If they want my brain, they can have it. But it'll be no good."

The girl cupped her friend in her hand.

"Let's beat them at their own game."

"What do you mean?"
"I need you to bite me."

The spider leapt away in terror, her dolor complete.

"How could you ask me such a thing! Besides, my fangs are poisonous, but they rarely cause death."

"I'll die if you bite me on the inside!"

The spider shuddered, for she knew it was true.

"You can't leave me all alone. You're all I have left!"

"What kind of friend will I be after tomorrow? This is the only way I can get out of here and stay me."

The spider agreed, on one condition.

***

The girl's death was unexplainable. All deaths signs were congruent with the venom of a brown recluse spider, yet no marks were found on the body, and such deaths in North America are rare.

The nurse who found thought she saw a spider crushed in the patient's fist. It clung to the girl's hair with an intensity that could only be attributed to love.

The nurse wiped the spider away, and dismissed the thought.

NORTH VS SOUTH

Once upon a Patriarchy, in a North-Side penthouse/bunker in The Big City, two attractive, rich, thin white women were having an argument.

One was a daughter: eighteen, golden blonde, blemishless, restless.

The other, her mother: forty-one, ash blonde, tummy-tucked, caffeinated.

The daughter's name was Emma; the mother's name was Isabelle.

Emma threw a vase from its shelf: a mild tantrum compared to her younger years.

"But I wanna go!"

"I simply will *not* allow it!" Isabelle stomped her eight-hundred dollar shoes: a pittance in light of her usual shopping sprees.

"You said once I graduated from high school I could do whatever I want!"

"I thought you'd want to marry a CEO, become an Instagram model! I didn't think you'd want to go to *university*!" Emma's mother wrung her diamond-crusted fingers. "Do you *really* need to think more?"

"Mom…!"

"You *do* know what happens when a girl *thinks* too much, don't you? She cuts off *all* her hair, becomes a *lesbian*, and *dies*!"

"Mom!!!"

"Do you *want* to die, Emma? Do you *want* to be a *lesbian* prostitute living below 121 Street? Do you *want* to wear *second-hand clothing*?!?!"

Emma pouted on their ten-thousand dollar couch. Isabelle continued her tirade, hoping to shock her daughter out of any dangerous ambition.

"Thinking is the most dangerous thing a girl could *ever* do! Why, even this *conversation* is making me think too much! Now I'll get age lines, and your father will leave me, and *then* where will we be?!?!" she rattled her diamond hoops. "*Enjoy* life, Emma. Leave thinking to the *poor*!"

The mother smiled, inspired, and eager to placate.

"Can't we send you to one of those *nice* Parisian schools in Switzerland?"

"I don't wanna go to Switzerland!"

"Would you like a *puppy*? I can send the maid down to one of the puppy mill pet stores…!"

"I don't wanna puppy, mom! I wanna go to university!"

"So you *do* want to become a lesbian! And *die*!"

"It's not like that, mom! The university isn't the academic institution it once was!

"I don't *care* about religion, I just don't want you to *think* too much!"

"I won't! It's a big party school."

Isabelle considered this.

"A party school?"

"Lots of sex, drugs, and reckless drinking."

Isabelle pondered.

"But what about the *poor* people?"

What *about* the poor people? Emma was even more clueless than her mother.

Luxury drops you dangerously close to indifference. Poverty's bad for body temperature regulation, attention span, veinal nutrition levels and maintaining sanity, but money's worse for everything else.

Except for taking cabs. Having no money means you have to walk, hitchhike, sneak onto the bus, or threaten the cab driver with a household utensil. Upper class transport is a breeze, which almost makes the damned soul worth it.

A taxi pulled up in front of the university. Emma handed the driver an unhealthily healthy wad of cash, remembered her entitlement, and grabbed back half.

After three days on campus, Emma was an anarchist.

(And asexual.)

SKIN DEEP

I've been training for the Scale-A-Thon since I was eight.

I know what you're thinking. Most kids dream of getting onto the National Fuck-Off or marrying a hologram.

A Scale-A-Thon's not the fast track to fame, but a test of endurance, a chance to make a difference. When you get up on the Scaleist Podium, you're provided a telepathic instamitter and can say ANYTHING you want.

For fifty seconds, the whole world will be listening, and I can finally tell them the truth.

It's not as morbid as my femme guardian says. The Scale-A-Thon isn't just about peeling away your flesh.

It's about scaling down to your soul.

People barely believe in souls anymore, but I do. The soul is what keeps us stirring inside. The soul is what makes us try.

The soul is what made me jump through the roof when I found out I qualified to race.

"Eff? Effy!"

I run screaming through our quarters with glee. My femme guardian's at the table, reading the news in her brain, drinking a hot cup of caffeine.

"I did it! I'm going to race the Scale-A-Thon!"

"Oh dear, not this again!" she blinks to skip to a new story.

"Anything new in the world?"

"Too many things."

"I can't wait to get my phone downloads when I'm nineteen!"

"Hmm." she rubs her head.
"What's down, Effy?"

"Nothing, hun. Just overwhelmed."

"Is it 'cause of Emmy?"

She tries to smile.

"Among other things."

"Do you want me to upload an app for you?"

"No, no, I'm fine."

"Okay. I'm going to go practice."

"My idol!"

"Don't swear!" I tease.

"You're always practicing!"

"The Scale-A-Thon is in seven days!"

"Wouldn't you rather relax with some nice VR?"

"Eff! This matters to me!"

"But why, darling? Why?"

I wish I could explain to her, or anyone, but a normal life isn't enough for me. I wish it were. I could become a Graphics Consultant or Space

Engineer, but I want my creations to last. I don't need anyone to know my name, but need my message out there.

That's why I practice. Every day, I cry, sweat, bleed. Every day, I'm rejected, ignored. But I can't stop, because one of these days, everyone will understand why I fought so hard in the first place.

It's been ten years.

I can wait another week.

***

I don't expect Effy to come watch. She doesn't get it, and besides, she hasn't left the house since my masc guardian…

Oh, Emmy. Dear, sweet Emmy.

I'm okay going out on my own. Most people are too busy inside their heads to care what's happening on the outside. I'm the same, in my own way.

The Scale-A-Thon will be held in the Founder's Auditorium, just fifty seconds away on the air-train.

Fifty seconds.

No time at all, but it could change everything.

There are mostly culture-addicts in attendance, but there's some younger crowd members, too, including two Iota fans for whom having their phones wired into their heads wasn't enough- they replaced their hands with phones, too.

I hear them chatter,

"Oh my idol! Is that…?"

"Auto-totes! It's Kay Kay!"

"Sandy Kay Kay?!"

"OMI! OMI! Kay Kay, Kay Kay, you're sooo hyper-lit!"

Sandy's fans start blinking out selfies. She flashes her smile (which is TOTALLY holographic! Can't they tell? Do they care?)

"Sandy! Sandy!" cries the first fan. "What'll you say if you get on the podium?"

"Oh, you know," Kay Kay ensures they get her best angle, "I'm just going to thank my radtacular fans, and my sponsor, Kinkster Interiors, providing you with all your kinky furniture needs. Have you heard of their new Thralldom Bondage Chair? Perfect for a public prison or private event!"

I bee-line to the Prepatory Rooms. Nobody's waiting to shake my hand- yet.

Most of the racers are old-timers: previous winners who make a living from re-plays of their fifty-second instalments. These are my celebrities. For a moment, they became the voice of their generation.

It's my turn.

Sandy Kay Kay is among three Iota models to throw their scalp into the ring. The Scale-A-Thon's gotten trendier than I realized.

We're equipped with gas masks so the acid-air doesn't get into our lungs. (When it first began, the Scale-A-Thon didn't necessitate face protection, resulting in multiple lawsuits.)

Everyone has turbo boots or speedster onesies. I have my Grand-masc progenitor's motorized scooter, from back when people's phones weren't downloaded into their heads. Grand-masc always said things were simpler then- maybe even better.

Our presiding hologram is the prettiest I've ever seen. They're andro, anthropomorphic, and their smile's loud enough to fill the auditorium.

I break out in sweat. Everything I've worked for is converging in this moment. Finally, fate is on my side.

Nobody believes in fate anymore, but I've seen it work.

"Here we are, femmes and fembots!" the hologram sends off sparks with their perfect hair. "It's the cultural event of the year! The Scale-A-Thon, brought to you by Skin Shave incorporated!"

That podium is mine.
"Marks, set, go!"

We break through the shield into a biting atmosphere.

I leave everyone behind. The old-timers are slower each year; the models are too busy posing to care.

This is what I'm here for.

This is what I was born to do.

The faster you go, the more the acid-air shaves your skin. I'm so used to the burn by now I barely notice. I am a snake. I am built to shed. I am made to bear my insides to the world.

I didn't expect it to reach so deep.

My epidermis is gone. I'm a shiny, burning slab of pink.

My skin is a flag flying behind me, no doubt spraying magnificent, patriotic blood.

My muscles are next. If I don't reach the end fast enough, I'll have nothing to kick with.

This is the price we pay for looking within. The road to enlightenment never did run smooth, nor safely.

One of the old timers is catching up with me: Bek Torrents, three-time champion. I want to tell her, "I love your work!", but she wouldn't hear me over the roar.

She veers into my lane, and slows down right in front of me.

Then, she stops.

I don't know what to do. Everyone else remains far behind, but I can't risk them catching up. As I slow down, the astringent zephyr cools on my melting face, burning more now that I'm staying still.

I can't run over my inspiration!

Can I?

The stadium is an echo chamber of chants. I can hear one chant above the rest:
"Kay Kay! Kay Kay!"

Nobody knows me. Nobody cares.

This is my only chance.

My shins start to bubble. I can't wait any longer. I rev my engine in warning and speed around Bek, leaving her to eat my dust (and blood.)

I'm sweating buckets of it. This is a high like no other. I always told Effy I ignored the pain, but I love it.

Pain is what connects me to my passion.

There's no feeling like crossing the finish line. You crash back to the other side, and fresh, clean, loving breeze blasts your face anew.

My skin snaps back in place. Like all torture, it was impermanent, and well worth fifty seconds on that podium.

"I did it! I did it! I won!!!"

The hologram waves in recognition. I can't hear the cheers over the screaming in my chest, the blood rushing in and out my ears.

The medics test my vitals while we await the remaining competitors.

"Your skin will be loose for a few days. Drink plenty of electrolytes!"

I beat everyone by a landslide.

After we've all gathered, I await my accolades.

"Thank you, everyone! We are pleased to present this year's first place to…"

This is my moment...!

"Sandy Kay Kay, Iota model and proud brand slave for Kinkster Interiors!"

I wish my skin were off again. Anything to distract me from the terror of losing.

"Excuse me? Excuse me!" I push my way to the podium, where Sandy's crying like she just won Miss Milky Way. "There's been a mistake!"

The hologram smiles down on me.

"Is there a problem?"

"Yes, there's a problem. I won first place. You were there. You saw it."

"You were in an eleventh lane. There are only ten lanes permitted in the Scale-A-Thon. You must have created your own lane to cheat the race."

I've never felt an adrenaline rush like this- not even when I was bullied into sipping pure adrenaline.

"What? No! I didn't know! I'm properly registered! I completed the race fair and square! And I did it better than anyone! I deserve a place on that podium!"

The hologram is unmoved.

"Please make way for the winner."

"No! Please! I worked harder, and I care more! I have something to say!"

"That's not what the podium is about."

I've never argued with a hologram before. They remain annoyingly amiable.

"Then why did you let me race? Why did you make me go through all of this?"

The hologram grins all the more, perhaps in sympathy.

"To be honest, we barely noticed you."

***

I'm outside the stadium on the edge of the commute lanes, secretly wishing someone's transport would run me over. Crushed on another starless night.

"Hun?"

I'd know that voice anywhere. She's my last connection to the real world.

"Effy?" my throat breaks. "Mom?"

She laughs in surprise.

"You haven't called me that since…!"

"Well, it's not the way anymore."

"Of course." she smiles. "But it's nice to hear."

I wish I could peel myself off the curb for a hug, but all my energy was lost chasing a star.

Our reach is so far, and our grasp so small.

If you lose, you can't re-enter the Scale-A-Thon for ten years.

I had my chance. Now it's gone.

"I can't believe you came!"

"Of course I came! I wouldn't have missed it for a condo on Mars!"

"I'm sorry I let you down."

"No, I'm sorry."

"What are you sorry for?"

She sits; we're both defeated now.

"I'm the one who got you in the eleventh lane."

"What?"

"I looked up your file. They were going to reject you, so I bribed a bit, hacked a little, and got you an extra spot. They said they'd overlook it. But I guess the hologram had other plans."

I don't need more epiphanies tonight. Or ever.

"So I didn't even get in on my own merit?"

"Oh hun, you deserved a chance in this race! It doesn't matter how you got in! Didn't you see how well you did? You should have won. I'm the one who ruined it for you."

"Honestly?" I stared back at the stadium, full of new fans screaming Sandy's name (and singing the Kinkster jingle.) "I'm pretty sure it was rigged either way."

Losing was one thing. Now I have to contend with the consequences.

I didn't apply to any universities, virtual or irl. I have no jobs lined up.

I have nothing.

"What will I do now? Ship off to the Fun Farm?"

"You'll have another chance! I don't know why the race matters to you so much, but…"

"It's not the race I care about!" I tremble with the terrible truth. "It's the podium."

"What's so important about the podium?"

"It's my only chance to be heard! You can't post anything anymore unless it has sponsored content! I just… wanted to share my words with the world."

"Well," she squeezes my shoulder, "what would you have said?"

"I wanted to tell everyone…"
"Hang on!" she blinks. "Let me set a timer. Okay. You have fifty seconds. Go!"

"Life is worth more! More than three second snaps, more than plug-ins or auto-ads. I wanted to remind people they matter. Each person has something special, not just their face or their brand potential, but something real, something deep down inside that's so hard to reach these days.

Maybe it's not the soul. Maybe souls really are obsolete. But there's something about us that's so worthwhile. It's what made Grand-masc give me his scooter. It's what made Emmy… Dad… fight 'til the very end. It's what makes you and I miss them. And it's what keeps us together when everything's falling apart.

That's what I hurt for, work for. I want a chance to wake people up."

"Time's up." she blinks to turn the alarm off. "Well. That was a great fifty seconds! Well worth waiting for."

I pick myself up.
"Even ten years?"

"Longer than that! We'll find a way. You'll see."

We head home, but take our time, in case my skin falls off on the way.

SUICIDE NOTE #2

I love people so much and hate them in turn. I do believe love will win because love doesn't need to fight.

Please take any money and donate to a mental health service or wherever may help make help accessible.

Please text everyone on my phone to let them know. Same w FB/email. I don't want anyone to think I forgot them.

I love everyone so much. I wish I were well, or better yet, brave.

I am so so sorry. Everyone always says they want me to be okay. Maybe that's not the point.

Please get my books published. Please sell my unrecorded songs to be performed by others. Please do not waste money on burial. Cheapest option, please. I would personally love to be composted—if that's a thing. Please make a Hurt Heals art installation, of my art and other art submissions—all proceeds to mental health support groups.

Tiger to L when she's old enough. Diaries published. J gets white water bottle, J** gets pink. Pls donate guitar to an inner city art group in Deadton. Heirlooms (coffee table, kitchen table) for the family. Books to whoever wants/needs. M, you can keep for your used bookstore.

I am very sorry. I love you all. I wish love paid bills. I wish love could put out this terrible fire in my mind. I wish the voices would stop. I wish people were kinder. I wish C****** S****** said sorry. I wish I could forgive her.

I wish people liked my writing/music/etc. I wish artists had the means to support each other. I wish my balcony was tall enough.

I love you all. I am so grateful for every last moment. I know some have lashed out at me from their own pain but I do not want to leave in bitterness and victimhood. I want to forgive fucking everyone, EVERYONE. I have this head no matter the "kindness of strangers."

O my loves! Music and musicals. Birds and bumblebees and lilacs. We can do this. We needn't choose love. Love chooses us.

I know the world will go on beautifully. The world does not need me and I am glad. This "I" may need this world, but I am sure "I" is but a fragment of my wholeness. I know not if this wholeness can ever be found in life or death but I trust love. There is love even in sorrow, or pain, or death. In every tear is a pinch of happiness. I am pregnant w love for the world. The world is my baby. I do not need to watch you grow up. You will do just fine, my baby bird.

I wanted to do really great things. But only love is great. Why compete w God? I was very silly. How could I be a best seller or chart hit or filmmaker? The truth is I am too much in love with kissing flowers, hugging trees, humming prayers.

I am sorry my love is so useless on the material plain but I hope all my smiles at strangers did something. Made someone's day.

Maybe even saved a life.

ARCHER'S PARADOX

Cupid's arrows oft fly amiss.

In days of yore, he kept to shepherd's fields and ocean shores, where people were simple, good, and otherwise equipped to weather love's rigours.

Now he frequents bars, apps, and anywhere else guaranteed to make love impossible.

Vacationing in the Big City, Eros made another mistake, one for which Fidel was bound to suffer more than the mythological matchmaker.

Fidel was the security guard at the King's Hovel back when the South Side had electricity. He looked the part: big and tall with a sensitive side he was prohibited to show.

Darla looked her part, too: all curves and curls with a face made prettier by fake lashes and soft lighting.

What inspired Cupid to fire at 1:35 in a dive bar on a Tuesday? In his defence, it was a fine fall day, which, though lacking the juvenescence of spring, possessed a charm in which everyone felt aligned, grounded, and at the right place. This was true for Fidel and Darla—or would be if Cupid had any say.

 He braced his bow while his targets chatted about the weather.

"You drinking?" Darla offered.

"Not on the job," Fidel conferred.

"Oh, come on—" she strutted her stuff all the way to the bar, which wasn't far, but it had the right effect.

"I wouldn't," warned Zhi, Fidel's boss, and friend. "She's got that look."

Cupid wasn't about to let reason ruin his fun. When Darla returned with a round of tequila slammers, he landed his bullet.

A week later, Darla moved in.

She seemed sweet, at first. Most humans do. But her saccharine surface melted out, only enhancing the acridity in Fidel's own heart. It was, in all respects, a Swipe Left situ.

Swiping Left only works in that illusory dimension humans have hacked together. In reality, people get stuck. Maybe that's why they opt for the unreal.

Fidel would work until two and come home to find the dishes unwashed, a meal unmade, laundry piled up. Darla alleged to be looking for work, but he never saw resumes, or heard of any callbacks, let alone any interviews.

He'd wash the dishes, make a meal, load the laundry, and wait for his capricious paramour to stumble in at 4 AM.

"Where were you?" he'd ask.

"Nowhere," she'd reply.

"Who is he?" he'd ask.

"No one," she'd reply.

But she'd been everywhere, with everyone.

Cupid didn't worry—when an arrow didn't fit, it fell out on its own. It always hurt but left the heart open for the next disaster.

The sensuous seraphim was determined to find the right girl for Fidel. Or guy? Nope, Cupid concluded. This one was straighter than Babel.

He scoured the Big City for the ideal match; someone who could withstand Fidel's woes.

Then he set his trap.

Every Saturday once he'd left Darla, Fidel went for a walk. The local library loomed invitingly, but he always passed by—until the day Cupid left the door open.

Fidel was duly tempted.

Libraries used to be beautiful. The modern monstrosities imprison great minds behind endless walls of glass. This ancient atheneum was three stories of hefty bindings, spiral staircases and creaking wood, reminiscent of another time, demanding a reverence no librarian could invoke with a hush. Fidel was inspired to procure an arm chair and a pipe for his newfound love affair with literature.

Then he saw her.

She looked the part, not of a lover, but a bookworm. She even wore glasses, to Fidel's (and Cupid's) delight.

Fidel wasn't used to libraries, which is probably why he leaned on a bookcase that was no good for leaning, which replied with a wibble, wobble, and pile of books on the floor.

He awaited a fury of raging cataloguers, but Amanda came to his rescue.

A meet-cute! Perfect! Cupid watched and waited.

"Oh. I'm so sorry. It's such a mess—"

"Yeah," Amanda laughed, "it is!"

"Let me help…"

"I got it, I got it."

"Are you a librarian?"

"Don't have the degree. I'm a glorified bookshelfer. Can I help you find something?"

"Uh…" Fidel made a desperate search in the pile. "Henry James! Yeah. I'm mad about Henry James."

He knew nothing about Henry James.

"Yeah? You read that one?"

Fidel chanced a glance at the title.

"Why, no. Not this one. At least, I can't recall. You?"

"Yeah. Loved the beginning. Hated the ending," she scoffed at her own candour. "Guess I just ruined it for you!"

"No worries. Anything you'd recommend?"

She shot around the corner to return with a maroon hardcover eaten at the edges.

"Here. The only happy ending Edith Wharton ever wrote. Rare in romances."

"You got that right." Fidel took the book, "I've never seen them end in anything but fire and brimstone. Whatever brimstone is."

"Uh—sulfur, I think."

"Sure. Fire and sulfur. Sounds like a cakewalk compared to my love life. I don't even know why I came in here. Like a book can solve the problem of love! Oh, don't mind me. I'm just a broken idiot spoiling your day."

Fidel couldn't believe it: was he confiding to this bookshelfer? The way people embarrass themselves in front of bartenders?

Much to his surprise, and relief, Amanda was compassionate.

"You're not broken. Not yet."

"Still an idiot."

"Maybe. I don't know you. Yet."

Her smile looked like a promise.

Cupid rallied. He remained optimistic (or maybe he was drunk). Either way, he plunged another arrow through Fidel's battered heart, which at this point resembled a pin cushion.

Fidel felt brave. Maybe it was all the fresh air. Maybe it was Edith Wharton, or Henry James. Either way, he asked Amanda out.

Amanda felt free. Maybe it was because she only had an hour left of her shift. Maybe it was all the Edith Wharton she'd been reading. Either way, she said yes.

It dawned on Cupid that apps didn't work because you had to actually be with a person to be with them.

Amanda and Fidel were destined a beautiful future were it not for their past. The past is never far behind. Especially when it comes to love.

Fidel monopolized their first date divulging his tragedy. By their third month, Amanda knew the story by heart, so much so it felt like a novel penned by her favourite writer or someone equally depressing.

Darla was an adamant ghost, almost good enough to win the title "stalker." She texted, phoned, Snap-chatted, and DM'd so much Fidel had to turn off his notifications. Of late, her messages had turned to threats, not for his physical safety, but her own.

Despite this red flag big enough to bait a bull, Amanda was lovestruck. Fidel was funny, smart, and actually liked to read beside her in bed. If they wanted to move forward, she'd have to help him leave Darla behind.

"Ever thought of blocking her?" she inquired one day over brunch.

Fidel contemplated his mimosa, "I don't know. It feels like it's never done."

"You should write her a letter."

"Should I?"

"I did it for all my exes. You don't have to send it, but it helps clear the air. And the heart."

"Yeah," he sniffed in that way men do to pretend they can't cry. "Maybe one day."

He never got to write that letter, or at least send it. For one of Darla's suicide bluffs proved true.

He didn't go to the funeral. He couldn't.

He couldn't do anything anymore.

A week later, Fidel moved in. As Fidel said himself, "I'm a mess without you."

Amanda was happy to help.

She had her own heart holes: a creepy uncle, abusive boyfriend, some hateful lovers, some rape-y "friends." Yet, she was that rare human who took her hurts as reason to help others heal.

She sometimes shut down from his moods (thanks to the abusive boyfriend), or froze at his touch (credit to the creepy uncle), but compared to Fidel's karmic burdens, Amanda travelled light.

Fidel was ruined over Darla—whether more over her life or death, it was unclear. He kept Amanda, but lost everything else.

Days gestated to weeks, weeks matured into months, months aged into years.

When people asked Amanda about children, her favourite retort was, "Don't need any—I have him!"

After a while, it stopped being funny.

She'd come home to dishes unwashed, a meal unmade, laundry piled up, and after a while didn't even wonder where he was. She knew he was in the study.

When he first requested the space, she was glad. She'd elected it as a workout room, a moot point due to her gym membership. This way, he had a space of his own. It made the apartment feel like a home for them both.

Early in the morning, she'd coax Fidel out of the office for breakfast.

Late at night, she'd pull him from the office into bed, and later still, she'd wake up alone again.

What was he doing in there? Writing. Not typing, writing. Paper shuffled, pens scritched and scratched and sometimes broke from their master's furor.

People often wonder why couples stay together when they're so wrong for each other. The answer is often sex.

Sex is the string that ties love's arrows tight. When done right (or, you could argue, wrong), its fog is thick enough to blind us to our actions and their consequences—namely, the choice to stay with someone who is more of an idea than a reality, and the resentment that builds on that denial.

Sex helps us bide time—and kill it. To this day, physical intimacy remains the most frequently abused drug in society (human or otherwise), and has claimed the most lives, if only day by day.

It was Valentine's Day: Cupid's most-loathed holiday. He thrashed through the Hallmark-pink sea of fuchsias, salmons, roses, corals, flamingos, bubblegums, and blushes (Cupid is a Winter, benefitting from blue, black, and white hues).

Even worse, 78% of his attributed matches were a mess, the remaining 22% too deluded to count as successes. The only pleased partners were those who consciously coupled, but if everyone activated self-awareness in the love realm, he'd have to find a new hobby.

What the hell was the point of loving anyone? Cupid mused. Why pour your heart out to one person when a heart's better shared with the world?

Cupid especially pitied Amanda. It was his fault. For sure as he molly-whopped Fidel, Amanda's bulls-eye was smashed through.

Valentine's was on a Saturday, and when Amanda woke up late, Fidel was gone. Not in the office; she knocked to find no one. So she wandered her apartment, somehow emptier since her lover moved in.

Cupid used his heart-vision to assess her vascular status.

Her heart was huge, but going hollow.

How could he let this happen? If humans couldn't be trusted to fall in love on their own, how could he expect them to fall out of it?

He had to break her heart if only to help her get it back.

So, he set another trap.

Humans are easily tempted. As Cupid had always known, most anyone needs is a door slightly open.

Amanda noticed sunlight pouring out of the office. For five years, she'd ceded that territory, and now, she was compelled to reclaim it.

It reminded her of the library: woody and rich, odorous with ink and dead trees.

A room devoted to words.

There were pages on pages on stacks on piles on pages.

They were scattered and strewn about like rude, naked books.

They spilled from every drawer.

They filled every shelf.

They gave the floor a new carpet.

She picked up one piece of the puzzle. Then another. Her eyes flitted; her hands shook.

The letters made words, the words crammed pages, and each page amassed to a chapter of a seemingly endless book.

Every article, every syllable, every sentiment was for Darla.

Longer than any Edith Wharton, with an ending even more tragic.

Cupid sighed,

"If only you'd met in the 10th century! You'd have been a perfect match then!"

Fidel entered his office, surprised by his partner's intrusion.

"Oh. I'm so sorry. It's such a mess—"

Amanda brandished a page.

"Yeah. It is."

"Manda…"

"This is what you've been doing all this time? Writing a thousand-page love letter?"

"No!" Fidel cringed. "It's a story. Our story. Mine and hers."

"So while I've been trying to make a life for us, you've been dwelling on the one you had with her?"

"No, it's just—"

"For Christ's sake, Del! It's Valentine's Day!"

"I know." he produced a limp bouquet all the more impotent in his shrine's midst.

She grabbed the roses (red—her favourite) and smashed them against the monolith manuscript.

She left him with Darla's letter, rose petals on the floor.

***

That night, Fidel patroned his former workplace. It was the first time he drank there since that fateful fall day that could have set him on an entirely different path, had he been in control.

Fidel wasn't in control much these days.

Zhi, no longer a boss, but still a friend, lent an ear to the twisted tale.

"Why did you do it? You had to know she'd leave you!"

"I couldn't help it. She asked me to."

"She told you to write a letter, not a goddamn tome!"

"Not Manda. Darla."

"What do you mean?"

Cupid knew Fidel would spill eventually, but thought he'd tell the truth to the one who deserved to hear it.

Too many keep their secrets on the inside, and only save their pearls for pigs.

Same for their devotion.

"I'd come home, and Darla would be there. Go to bed, there she was. She was always asking me to write our story down. She said once the story was finished, we could rest," his hands did nothing to iron out his wrinkles. "I'm so, so tired."

"But—Darla's dead."

Fidel trembled, first with terror, then sobs; his friend could only watch.

"That was always the problem with Darla! I could never say no. And she would never give up."

Zhi didn't know what to say except,

"Did you finish it?"

Fidel took his last sip.

"Yes. Right after Amanda left."

The broken man broke his pint by dropping it off the partition. It landed with a splash, smashed in two. He fell off his stool, and nothing could help him back up.

Cupid winced. This was his fault, too. He hadn't realized before, but Darla's arrow had gotten stuck.

All this time, it had burrowed deeper.

It was fused to Fidel's spine as well as his soul.

"It was always her," Fidel cried, clutching a heart no longer his. "It's always been her!"

SHARING SPACE

"I can't feel the weather."

"Whaddya mean?"

"I can't tell what the weather's like!"

"Chrissake, Lorde," Ang rolled her eyes. "There's no weather in space."

True. The bay's internal temperature was set to a boring twenty degrees Celsius. Better than freezing/sweating your balls off, but Lorde craved variation.

For all its dangerous repute, space-pirating was a bore.

This (ad)venture had lasted two weeks, starting at Ritter's Port 'til Here-ish, wherever Here was, and they'd yet to spot any ships worth pillaging.

Lorde worried pirating was a poor career choice.

"I'm homesick."

"Home doesn't exist."

True. Lorde's galaxy imploded well after Lorde's ancestors hopped their space-jet: the first inter-galactic colonists. They'd started on Mars, then sought the great black yonder, but rumour was, before Mars, there was Earth.

Lorde had never seen Earth, but as it turned out, you didn't need to know something to miss it.

"I wanna go home."

"Come off it! Your great-granddaddy was one of the first space settlers. Ya'know the song: *Born to ride the starry frontier…*"

"I know…" Lorde wished Ang wouldn't sing.

"So be proud, ya little—" Ang's verbal assault was silenced by a beeping monitor.

Lorde knew little about space ships, but knew certain monitors shouldn't beep. Ever.

"Ah, shit!" Ang trembled. "Ghost bones!"

"No way!" Lorde trembled back. "That's all mythology!"

"Don't you know ANYTHING?" Ang asked like it was a serious question. "All those damn Earthlings you miss so much shot all their dead kin into space. Now we're stuck with the ghosts. Thanks a bunch, Earth-idiots!"

This pissed off Ang's first mate.

"You talk like you ain't one of 'em!"

"I ain't! I am of Space. I'm all about Space. Shit, Lorde! Is it so hard to accept I'm happy?"

"You don't seem happy," said Lorde (under his breath, of course).

WrrrrRRRRRRRRRIP.

The lights clicked off. Then on. Then off again.

"Gabe?" Ang tried the PA, "Gabe, what's with the engines?"

"Mufflemufflmrsted," replied Gabe through the radio.

"Shit."

Click.

Lorde's panic was perfect and complete. Breath was extraneous.

Ang couldn't have cared less, "Buck up, kid! I'ma check on Gabe. Wait here. Hold down the bay. If you see any ghosts, scream."

Lorde was not planning on waiting, or screaming, or holding down the bay. His thoughts more so fell along the lines of, "What's the most painless way to commit suicide?" and, "Why did Ang even recruit me?"

Lorde remembered the day destiny introduced itself as Ang (easy to remember: it had only been two weeks). Lorde was chilling in the Ritter's Port dining hall, pretending to look for a job. Ang walked in, and that was it.

Some people don't need to do more than walk.

"You prolly only hired me 'cause of my great-granddaddy," Lorde grumbled (but only after Ang left).

Crrkkkcrrkkk said the beeping monitor. That didn't sound great.

Hheeeeeeeepppphhh… That sounded even worse.

Hhhheeeeeeellllllllppppp meeeeee—

"OH SHIT!" Lorde said, and when the PA blasted screams from the engine deck, he added, "Motherfucker," and "Fuck this!"

"The ghosts are crying for help and the ghosts are killing my friends and oh shit motherfucker fuck this!!!!!!" and after all that, including the exclamation points, he ran.

Funny thing about Space: there's nowhere to run. You can only run from the bay to the sleep pods to the storage space to the engines, but then again, people were SCREAMING down there—but there Lorde's feet went, and on the way he grabbed a pipe, the kind Ang bent into interesting shapes to intimidate rich people with, and when the engine room came into view Lorde learned madness tasted like tin and made you pray.

"Please oh please oh please oh please…"

Lorde didn't know what lay at the end of this request, but it felt important.

The door creeeeeeeaked, which only made matters worse.

What used to be Gabe was a puddle near the garbage-burner.

Lorde vomited lunch (and breakfast).

Then SOMETHING grabbed his shoulder and it took him a while to realise it was him screaming this time.

"Chrissake, Lorde! It's me!"

"Ang? You're alive?"

"No, I'm a ghost you idiot!"

"What happened to Gabe?"

Ang grabbed Lorde's collar tight. Lorde tried to ignore all the blood. "We've gotta go."

"But…"

"Ya hear me?"

"How are we supposed to fix a dead ship without an engine expert?"

"Gabe was far from an expert. We'll do fine."

"Fine? How are we gonna do fine? Gabe exploded!"

Ang winced. "I know. I saw it."

"Was that you screaming? Was it Gabe?"
"Shut it!"
"I'm gonna be sick again."

***

Lorde wondered how there could be so much to vomit when breakfast AND lunch were already evacuated. Ang wondered what temporary insanity lead to this recruitment.

Then they wondered what the fuck to do about the ghosts.

"I'll boost the engines," Ang decided. "We'll high-tail outta here. Flag down the nearest ship. Ditch this baby and commandeer the next."

"We hafta ditch the ship…?"

"Once ghost bones hitch onto a ship, that's it. They're like… space lice! Only they explode your insides."

Lorde wondered why the ghosts hadn't gotten to work exploding THEIR insides, and asked.

"Dunno." Ang returned to the engines, eyeing the walls for potential foes, "Maybe they're full. 'Cause they ate Gabe."

Ang tip-toed over the gunk formerly known as Gabe and proceeded to hot-wire the ship. Lorde wondered what kind of childhood she had to prepare her for this.

Prrrrrrrrrrrrrrrrrw!—the engines hummed to life.

Ang used Lorde's shirt to wipe her hands.

***

Back at the bay, Lorde organised their mission into steps:

> Step 1. Track another ship.
>
> Step 2. Flag down ship.
>
> Step 3. Board ship.
>
> Step 4. Commandeer ship…?

"What are you doing?!" Ang tore up the page. "We gotta go! Boost our trackers! Set our coordinates!"

Lorde boosted and tracked and coordinates were set and the engine hobblewobbled into a speed resembling hyperspace and the nearest ship turned out to be the snottiest cruise they'd ever seen: a true pirate's holiday.

"Sweet!" Ang screamed, and checked their rocket packs for batteries.

Lorde stared at the mammoth machine above.

"Can you even fly that thing? Won't they have security? Won't they—"

"Get your helmet!"

***

Step 1. Track another ship. Check!

Step 2. Flag down ship. Check-ish?

Step 3. Board ship…

"Are you sure about this?" Lorde echoed under his helmet. "They don't look hitchhiker-friendly. Or pirate-friendly, for that matter."

"Pirates don't wait for invitations!"

Exit doors opened, and their rocket packs zizzled towards the cruise ship.

Lorde hated inter-space-connections. Your body seemed to echo. You became No one and Nothing, and though it only took one or two secs for bay doors to open and suck you in, those one or two breaths felt like the bus stop to Hell.

Ang *Woo-hooed* 'til they landed.

They aimed for what looked like a servant/cargo entrance, and entered what they hoped would be interpreted as an SOS on the key pad.

A voice enveloped their heads:
"State Worker-Code-Registration for Clearance Check. Over."

"For fuck sake…" Ang smashed the key pad with a pipe.

"Why did you bring that?!"

"I ain't walking into a cruise ship empty-handed," Ang grinned. "And I ain't leaving empty-handed, either."

Lorde never understood why Ang didn't hire lackeys, or thugs, or bodyguards—not until she smiled.

That smile did all the work for her.

Key pad busted, Ang tampered with the leftovers and Lorde wanted to start an Ang Cult because there was nothing better than a god who actually got shit done.

Sure enough, the entrance opened, and inside, a robot butler looked confused.

"Clearance Check Failure. Over. Repeat, Clearance Check Failure. Over. Please manually insert Worker-Code-Registration. Thank you. Have a nice—"

Ang smashed it in the face.

"So this isn't a covert mission." Lorde stared at the supine robot, who, until fixed, would boast an expression of permanent surprise.

Ang lead the way, high on violence. Lorde followed, full of trepidation.

"We're not really gonna steal this ship, are we?"

"We need a ship, don't we?"

"We're definitely on the security cameras. And there's definitely security guards…"

"Chrissake Lorde, don't you think I know that…?!"

Right on cue: guards with stun-guns who looked more like space-suit models. Come to think of it, the robot butler was cute, too. Rich people must like being surrounded by good-looking people, Lorde reasoned.

What would it be like to be on this cruise ship, instead of invading it? What would it be like to eat something other than powdered beans.

"Drop your weapon!" the burliest guard demanded.

"Hey, chill," Ang flashed that smile, "we're just late. We're caterers. Ain't we?"

"Yeah!" Lorde jumped in. "We cater."

H…heeeeeeh… said one of the guard's wrist-talkies. They looked at their wrist in confusion.

He…heeeeeeeeehlp…

"Oh shit." said Lorde.

The guards started to convulse. It looked like an epic dance party except everyone was in agony.

"The ghosts!!!" cried Ang. "The ghosts hitchhiked with us!"

Lorde would always remember the first time he saw someone's insides explode.

***

Lorde and Ang stood in a pool of bloody guts, trying to compose themselves.

"What a mess," Ang's hair dripped blood.

"I know," Lorde's nose dripped blood.

"The ghosts…"

"exploded…"

"all of them…"

They vomited (by this point Lorde could only puke stomach acid).

Lorde felt a breakdown coming on. Even Ang looked perturbed.

"What are we gonna do?"

"Chrissake, how would I know?"

"How did the ghosts come with us?"

"How would I know?"

"Why didn't the ghosts kill us?"

"I don't know, Lorde! We gotta kidnap the Captain and hi-jack this babe before the ghosts get us too!"

One look at a "Visitor's Map" from a very friendly hologram and they were off to see the Captain, who they knew would NOT be on the main decks, because on a ship like this captains have automated everything to do everything for them. The Captain would be sexually harassing people in the VIP lounge, sloshed on cosmo-cocktails.

Ang had a plan:

"You distract the Captain. Everyone knows you—at least after you explain who you are. I'll come up from behind and BAM!"

133

"You'll hit him with the pipe?"

"Nope— I'll hold a razor to his neck."

"Christ…"

"Chill, Lorde. Oh shit, wait!"

"What?"

"You can't distract the Captain. You have blood all over… everything."

Lorde remembered.

"Shit."

"Get in that hygiene booth! Quick!"

After a quick clean-up, the plan was back in action.

"Gosh, they had some fancy soap."

"That'll be the first room we pillage."

"We're gonna pillage our own ship?"

"Take a left!"

The place was oddly empty. Where were all the drunk, rich people being drunk and rich?

This question was answered by a shriek. A rich, drunk person smothered in blood ran downstairs, screaming,

"Oh please, oh please, oh please!!!" before they convulsed, screamed more, and exploded.

Lorde covered his face, which didn't help a bit.

"Damn," Ang observed the mess, "Just when we got you cleaned up."

Lorde wrung rich person blood out of his shirt.

"I will never, ever get used to seeing that."

"Look on the bright side! The ghosts are bumping off richies one by one!" Ang looked delighted, which was creepy considering the context. "This takeover will be easy!"

"Unless the ghosts get us too!"

"They haven't yet…"

"But *why?*"

Ang was never one to question good fortune.

On they ran. Past the sewage centre, garbage-burners, food atrium, servants' quarters, then up past the kitchen, the dining rooms, the cheesecake cafes and espresso bars, the jazz quarter, the dance halls, swinger bars, orgy room, gymnasiums, spas, tennis courts, VIP VRTL RLTY rooms, and, of course, an Earth/Mars Museum, with, apparently, a notable collection of juke boxes and baseball cards (whatever that meant).

The ghosts seemed to follow a different path, for the pirates witnessed no further carnage until they reached the lounge. They'd seen a few drunk, rich, un-exploded people, and merited shouts of, "We're calling security!" but, since Lorde and Ang knew most of security had exploded, they didn't worry.

They knocked the bouncer unconscious and burst through the doors.

The Captain looked like they were on their fifth cocktail—well ahead of schedule.

Lorde started, "Hello, Captain! I'm the great-grandchild of—"

Ang held a razor to the Captain's throat.

The ghosts weren't here: everyone was drunk and rich, and some people were pretty, drunk, and rich, and the bartenders were gorgeous and living on minimum wage, and it all seemed very nice and fine until two bloody pirates burst in to threaten The Captain.

"The nerve," a CEO tutted. Their friends tutted in agreement.

"What…" sloshed the Captain, "is the meaning of this?"

"We're taking over your ship," smiled Ang. "Take us to the navigation deck, or I'll slice yer throat and sic ghosts on yer friends! Whaddya say?"

The Captain looked at Lorde, perhaps with hope of intervention, "Who did you say your great-grandfather was?"

"…It's not important."

An awkward silence followed. Ang tried to expedite things by pressing the razor.

"Alright, alright!" The Captain caved. "I'll take you to navigation. Did you say something about ghosts?"

Heeehhhh…said the ship's speakers.

"What was that?" asked the Captain.

"Oh shit," said Lorde.

"The ghosts are gonna explode your guts unless you do what we want!" Ang looked mad with power. The drunk, rich people would have normally been too drunk and rich to care about this shit, but even they were interested.

"Don't tell fibs, Ang!"

"I never lied in my life! The ghosts are on our side!"

Hheeeeeellllllllp…

"Please!" The Captain begged. "Call off your ghosts!"

Ang to The Captain: "Give us the ship!"

Ang to the bartender: "Get me some rum!"

Lorde had never felt more homesick.

One of the CEOs started to jiggle, and the jiggles turned to convulsions, and people screamed, and Lorde wondered if it was possible to vomit your own stomach lining.

"Stop it!"

How can you reason with the dead? Why speak when no one will listen?

Fuck it.

"Please!" he tried again. Did the convulsion slow to a jiggle? "Stop exploding them!"

Hhheeehhhh?

The CEO dropped to the ground, unexploded.

Phew! Everybody relaxed. Even the Captain forgot they had a razor on their neck.

Any solace was interrupted by the appearance of a ghostface.

The average ghost would lose any beauty contest. This one was putrid. Sandpaper flesh all but scraped away. Mangled bones suffering an eternity in cold, passionless Space. The grinning, gutless visage made some richies faint and froze everyone else with fear but somehow, Lorde felt brave.

Hhhhheee....heeehhhh... 'scuse me. The ghost spat a chewy wad of phlegm. *That's better. Now, my child, why can't we get on with the killing?*

"Um..." Lorde was on the spot. "Why do you *want* to get on with the killing?"

The ghost's shoulders materialised so the ghost could shrug.

Gotta find some way to kill eternity.

All around, an invisible army answered with hollers, hoops and shouts.

I'm surprised you aren't more in our way of thinking. You and I are, after all, related.

(This may have been a Luke Skywalker moment if anyone had been privy to such an ancient pop culture reference.)

"What...?"

I'm your great-great-granddaddy. The first bones shot into space! Your great-great-granddaddy was the first space ghost, and your great-granddaddy was the first space pioneer. You are the lineage of legends! C'mon, let's get killin'.

"Is that why you didn't kill us?" Ang loosened her grip on the Captain. "'Cause Lorde's your descendant?"

Yep. The ghost grinned its lipless grin.

"What about me?" wondered Ang.

We like you. You got balls, girl.

"See, Lorde?!" Ang shouted in triumph. "Told ya you should be proud!"

Lorde exploded—and not by way of his guts. "I am NOT proud of such a violent heritage! I HATE that my great-granddaddy was the first space pioneer. Who knows how many peace-loving tribes he slaughtered throughout the stars? Who knows how many space-refugees my great-great-granddaddy's *exploded*? Space isn't meant to be conquered. It should be SHARED."

Words can do wonderful things. They can change minds, build bridges, tear down walls, cross boundaries.

This speech did nothing of the sort.

The rich people got mad because they felt attacked. The ghosts got mad because psycho-killers are naturally defensive. The Captain got mad about Ang and that razor. And Ang got mad at Lorde for ditching the plan.

The richies threw drinks, the bartenders ran, the ghosts exploded people willy-nilly, and the Captain and Ang started a game of who-gets-to-slit-whose-jugular.

Lorde was the eye of the storm, thinking along the lines of, "What would hurt more: a champagne bottle on the head, being throat-slit, or exploding?" Lorde went for the razor. Duck, duck, dodge, zip, into the middle of a two-person doggy-pile with a blade as the prize.

"Chrissake, Lorde, get off!"

"Kill me! Please Ang, kill me!"

"I'll kill you both!" The Captain screamed.

Ang slit the Captain's throat, which was messy, but given the surrounding carnage, made little change to the scenery.

Soon, the lounge was dead. Champagne flutes whistled. The bar dripped gallons of blood. Lorde stepped over disassembled guts, way past vomiting.

Lorde's great-great-granddaddy re-appeared, looking Zen.

See, Lorde? You can't sit around waiting for someone to share. Sometimes, Space needs to be TAKEN.

The ghost army revealed itself: ugly, bloody, and content. No one could have asked for a better crew on a giant pirate ship.

I was like you once, Lorde. I felt so alone, and all I could do was cry for help, and there was no one to save me! I realised I had to save myself—but we kept saying Help, 'cause it freaks people out.

The ghost crew chuckled. Ang looked full of admiration and awe, then looked at Lorde, and the expression stayed.

"C'mon, Lorde. Let's find the navigation bay. Set new coordinates. Whaddya say?"

Lorde looked at the blood, the bodies, the razor. The joyful glow in Ang's face. It was just like day they met, when Ang said, "Wanna be a pirate?" and Lorde said, "Okay."

"...Okay."

The ghost-pirates clapped. Lorde's great-great granddaddy bowed in respect. Ang took Lorde's hand, and lead him towards the future.

GET OFF

You always said I should sleep more.

So what if you left. Everyone does, one way or another. It is what it is.

Just gotta keep going.

My bus pulls out at 5:46. I find it funny when passengers call a bus "theirs" now that I'm driving one. It ain't theirs. It's mine.

It's all I have.

I'm running the Big City line all the way to Hippieville, ETA 43 hours, plus stops. That's nothing. I drove 37 hours *non-stop* when I moved back to the Big C. These bus lines underestimate me.

All you need to do is push yourself. If someone tells you there's a limit, it means they're too scared to cross it.

Maybe I crossed the line with you. You're sweet; you deserve better. Being with you made me a better person, while I only made you worse.

I knew it was over after your birthday. You didn't even try to kiss me.

I'm not perfect. But what about the good things? Like how I made sure the fridge was stocked with sugar-free Gatorade. Or how I never spanked you because you said it was triggering.

What about the sex? I thought you liked it.

I thought you liked me.

Why do I have to get a girl off to get her to stay.

Dammit. Forget it.

I've gotta get to work.

And I still haven't slept.

***

I've got this.

Another cup, another smoke, and I'll be good.

I hope the cat's okay. Best decision I ever made, rescuing her pretty face.

I've fucked up, I know, but you said it yourself: I'm a good person. I have problems same as anyone. So what if I get upset easily, or take a while to calm down?

After everything I've been through, it could be a lot worse.

I back out a bus stuffed with morons onto a road filled with idiots.

FUCKING DRIVERS. Does it ever occur to them a passing lane is for passing? I wish I had my bag of pennies to chuck, but I left them in my truck.

I need to start working out again. Anytime I go back home I gain five pounds. You told me I looked gorgeous, that I looked healthier than before, but all I can see is fat.

You always worried about me skipping lunch, but I have to. Otherwise, I can't stop. Not until it's all gone.

I can never go halfway.

Like with this route. Usually we'd trade off at Deadton. To hell with that. Who wants to leave a race before the finish line? Besides, we're understaffed. The powers-that-be seemed relieved when I told them I'd stick with it 'til the end.

141

Highway hypnosis is bullshit. It's not distraction—it's meditation! I get lost inside the road until some asshat rips me out of it with their lousy driving or idiotic questions like, "How far away are we from ___?" The adult version of "Are we there yet?"

There's a cutie onboard, but I have no interest in mixing business and pleasure. It's hard enough trying to schedule bathroom breaks.

Minutes, hours, days. Sleepless nights, angry mornings.

This is how I roll.

This is all I'll ever be.

***

I can do this.

Just another pill. Just another bump.

Bear hooks me up in Deadton. He only deals the best, and thank fuck, 'cause I'm all out of my prescriptions. Painkillers, Adderall, all gone. And they only work when I mix them.

I've deleted you from Facebook. I don't want to see your brown hair, smiling eyes, sweet lips.

When I say Goodbye, I mean it.

I feel like a sucker: showing your picture to my mom, inviting you to that wedding next summer. You said you were "emotionally invested," but couldn't go on without trying to "change me," which "isn't fair to either of us."

If you were that emotionally invested, how could you end it?

Bear can tell I'm down. Usually I keep my stories to myself, but this time I share.

"Don't let it get to you. On to the next! And, Scott buddy, you should really get some sleep."

He cuts me a line on the sink to test; we get chatty and piss each other off but soon all is forgiven, and I'm back to the bus with my pockets good and stuffed with the good stuff.

I'm gonna need every gram to get you out of my head.

The road's long, and lonely. Sometimes we hit scenery, but from now 'til Hippieville it's all flat-ass fields.

It makes my heart cringe.

It makes me think of our disastrous road trip.

I try to think of the future. But how can I when the past is so damn heavy? I wanted to take you away. I wanted you to have a good birthday.

I ruined everything.

I wonder what (or who) you're doing.

Do you miss me?

The road weaves.

I'm all out of pick-me-ups.

My teeth hurt. My stomach's worse. My head's a watermelon some dude karate-chopped.

Maybe you're right. Maybe I'm too hard on myself.

Maybe I should sleep more.

I'll just rest my eyes for a minute...

FIRST LAST TIME

It'll finally happen tonight.

I have it all ready: Silk sheets ($299 on Etsy). Red wine ('cause she hates champagne). Sexy Jazz Groove Spotify playlist, Woodwick candles, yes, even rose petals.

My modest basement suite is transformed into a sumptuous wonderland.

I can imagine her already. Shaved legs (or not—I'm not picky). Maybe she'll wear that vintage velvet dress she found at that night market on our first date, when she was stressed about midterms and ranting about Imperialism and I felt my dead heart hammer with the hope of newfound love.

We'll sit on the couch. She'll rant (I love her rants!), appraise the wine, shuffle the playlist beyond repair. Then we'll head to bed…

Her legs. That dress. Spread out in front of me.

The mere thought makes me salivate.

I check the wine glasses for marks. Rearrange the bouquet. Make war with the fridge magnets.

I'm totally whipped and I don't even care.

***

At 7 PM I'm doubting everything: shirt, menu, playlist.

When I see her through my peep hole, everything falls into place.

I was right about the rant: she's on a Voltaire kick. I listen happily while she paces/gesticulates, velvet hemline knocking weird, wonderful shadows on the walls while the candles sweat.

I was right about the wine, too. She sniffs, swishes, knocks back, and soon her swishes turn to spills and our giggles erupt into laughter and it looks like we aren't even going to make it to the bed.

Her kisses are my resuscitation.

It's growing. The heat. The thirst. The need. I feel it around her all the time, but now that we're alone, free to create our own melody, the whispers surge into a roar.

I will supplicate. I will prostrate.

I will get on my knees and pray.

I can feel her blood beat under her skin. She's pulling me closer, pulling me in.

My hand moves from her hair to her neck.

Most vampires dig their teeth into anyone with a pulse. I wanted to wait until I found the right person.

She's the one.

My teeth sharpen along with my tongue.

"Do you ever think about death?" I nibble her ear.

"All the time. Particularly how it pertains to the reunification of the subjective with the objective consciousness."

"What if there was a way to stop it?"

"Stop what?"

My fangs graze her skin. Vessels flutter. Blood ready to drip.

She's wet all over, inside.

"You want to live forever?"

"…Uh, not really?"

My fangs pull back. My lips go limp.

"What do you mean?"

"Well," she laughs a little, "it's depressing when you think about it. Imagine. You stay young forever, and all the people you love age and fade away."

I sit up. Sit back. My fangs have shriveled up.

"Uh, yeah, I guess you could say that."

"The times would change and you'd remember eras and customs long lost. You'd get jaded, or isolated, or worse, feel like you were better than everyone."

"Uh, yeah, I suppose that's possible."

"I mean, how could you even adapt to modernization?"

"Well," I pause Spotify, "that's easier than you'd think."

"But seriously, as far as hypotheticals go, it's one of the worst. Give me invisibility or the power of flight any day!"

"Flight? Seriously? You'd rather get gobbed with bug guts than live forever?"

"Well, taking into account common concepts of immortality, you're not actually living. You're dead. Ish."

"Yeah."

Her hand grasps mine: a hot coal on an ice cube.

"Your hands are always so cold! Here…" she blows warm kisses on my skin, but they'll never go as deep as I need them.

"Look, um, I think I got the wrong idea here."

"What? No! I'm totally enthusiastic in my consent."

"Maybe. But you're not consenting to what I had in mind."

It's hard telling someone you really like that you're dead.

She takes it well, all things considered.

"So, you wanted to—" she examines the rose petals and wine bottle anew. "Was this…?"

"Don't worry about it!"

"Were you…?"

"It's okay!"

"Oh, I'm so sorry!"

I'm whipped in more ways than one. Whipped by her, whipped by destiny. I try to avoid the brooding undead cliché, but right now, I'm up to my neck in self-pity.

"I feel like an idiot!"

"No, don't! It's kind of romantic! I'm just not ready for such a…long term commitment."

"Fair enough." I try not to stare at her jugular. "Honestly, a lot of what you said is true. Eternity isn't the best way to spend your time."

"Not alone, anyway," finished with the wine, she tastes my lips. "And I do love being with you."

I'd blush if my veins worked.

"Well then, do you want to be just a little immortal?"

"You can do that?"

"Sure. I take a little blood, you take a little of mine. We'd still be promised to each other, but you wouldn't have to do the whole permanent undead thing."

"Like…monogamish?"

"I guess. But with death."

She's on me, over me, legs and hips entwined.

"Sounds like a good compromise."

HIPPOCAMPUS, HACKS, AND HARDIHOODS

So I walk up an' slug 'im.

Went down like a bitch. Whimpered like one too.

Kids think they can make a name by running their mouth. No sense o' *sociability*. Hi-archy an' all. Kids like that need a slap, an' a hard one too.

Hi-archy an' anarchy are one in the same. Revolution's a temporary condition. When the dust settles, someone's gotta step in an' make sure shit works.

Burn what ya like; the system stays.

Society. Idiots ignore it, idealists fight it.

Idealists and idiots are one in the same.

Sin's a concept; attacking an idea's a waste a energy. I save my swings for real meat. You can't kill corruption 'cause it's in us with the blood, beer, streams a piss, an' scat. The world's broken, the break's *inside*, an' as long as there are streets to stain an' vermin like me to walk 'em, the mess'll always stay.

The Big City'll always be, 'cause it's in us. That's how we survive. Why fight the rules when you can win the game? Plenty to eat if you know who to jump, plenty to huff, hump, hit. Life's a pretty cement playground far as these beady eyes can see, an' there's no reason it or me should change.

The Hardihoods are the last gang to get it right. We only fight what we know'll bleed.

When you kick one down you drink it in, suck their humiliation dry. Eyes all on us, on *me*, hi-archy evident. Winner, loser. Fighter, bleeder.

"Damn—you went down faster than your mom!"

My boys roar in approval. Their laughter makes my eyeballs steam. I'm hot with the pleasure o' power, 'cause if the whole bar's mocking him it means they're praising me, so that's me king.

Kid turns his face up from the floor, tiny red eyes blinking pathetic tears.

Kids gotta know where they stand. One day they'll be put in their place, an' you can damn well bet I'm the one teaching them how to take it.

Kick 'im one more time, then ditch this dive. The boys follow behind, adding extra effect to my departure.

Always have some o' the boys with me. You gotta. They're an extension o' your own intimidation. You got collective height, muscle, *awareness*. Losers pretend the strength o' majority doesn't exist. Sad suckers. Not my fault I beat 'em to the punch—litterly.

Our victory march continues. Lights so high above remind me where we are and why. The Big City's the perfect place. It'll continue to crumble, and I'll be on top o' the rubble.

"Slitty, ma man!" someone slaps my back. I turn 'round to see some slime I keep for the drug connection. *Networking*, see.

"Sup," I kick a can. Best to fuck shit up whenever possible, remind everyone what you can do. When you got what I got, you can do near anything.

"Gotta tip!"

Kid's too eager, but my ears are perked. I guide him into an alleyway with one arm slung round, like brother, father, friend. Ha.

"Big one?"

"Huge, ma man," his teeth are grey. "Gotta pill staked out for ya."

A *whole* pill?! No wonder I keep this one 'round. I'm smarter than I look, even smarter than I think. I can see *potential*, an' that's a gift few got.

The deal's gonna go down on our territorial fringes. Rather it be in the heart o' our turf, but some days it's a shithead who makes the rules, an' if that shithead is the one with the drugs, even I gotta defer. Power's a fluid, currency. Take it, sure, but recognise it in others.

Even the most ruthless antrapener has to honour the transaction. Capitalism's booming better than ever, far as I can see; a score this big proves it. A whole pill could last a month, whether you're selling or storing.

The boys are as excited as me. They gotta be. They're just nervous 'bout leaving our hole. Long as feeling ain't a contagion, they can feel whatever the damn hell they want.

I'm too smart to be strung out on that stuff.

We sweep through the warehouse. I get Cull to stake out the perimeter, spread a few boys 'round, keep the rest behind me, where they belong. No more than five o' us; we won't need more. It's a big deal, but hardly a dangerous one.

Wood creaks. Baby bugs hatch in my chest. Like there's a fight between every class, a struggle up every ladder, there's always a weight to waiting.

Waiting's the worst. Us Hardihoods have a nasty relationship with time. We want its panties off, it wants another drink. With a bitch you can take what's yours, but you can't rape time any more than you can give your nightmares a black eye.

 Door opens. I stiffen. All my boys' shoulders go up with me, 'cause we breathe the same air, the same tension.

That's the kind o' loyalty I inspire.

It's the dealer an' one of his.

First you getta whiff o' what attitude the dealer expects, an' act accordingly. This one wants the job done with as little conversation as possible. Fine with that; hardly one for pleasantries.

Dealer's boy puts the briefcases in front, opens 'em click by click…

Holy fucking shit.

Each case has four pills each!!!! Muddy purple, mouldy blue, rotten egg-white. They're begging to be cracked, divided an' gobbled up by hungry, tripping heads.

These pills are so big I'd have to hold 'em with both hands!

"We're in business now," I grumble from the corner of my mouth.

One o' my boys flashes a dumb face.

"What are you talking about?"

"Shut it!"

An' he does.

When ya got power, you got people where you want 'em. Connections erupt, girls swoon, an' the circle feeds itself, friends for fucks, cash for friends, with powder an' pills to chase it all down.

Dealer finally speaks,

"Good?"

I mirror back his tight, uneven lips,

"Beaut." I'm so excited my bones have made a mosh pit, but I've gotta be *professional*.

Right when I'm about to make a signal for Bic to drop the money, there's a crash. Dealer's boy takes a dive to his jacket, ready for whatever. My head fills with ugly adrenaline. Some people would call it fear but it's my instincts surging.

A shape forms between empty boxes…

Bleach-white face…

Tiny red eyes…

It's the lil' bitch I socked in the bar!

"Well, well, what have we here?"

Kids think they can walk in wherever. How many times do you have to punch a boy down? As if I didn't already teach his face a lesson.

The Darkness is closing in, cornering the better parts o' my reasoning. Like too many before him, this lil' bitch has his cock up for revenge, but what he fails to understand is society *needs* losers, or the winners would be impossible to identify. Can't be called strong if there's no weakness to compare. Can't be better off if someone else ain't worse.

He snaps his fingers, an' I snap.

His boys erupt from the shadows, flooding us with knuckles. My boys scatter an' every face, body, an' soul blurs, identities lost as we become one with violence. The riot's alive an' I'm reborn with it. Every time I make contact with teeth or kick or slash or slap or punch or whack I hear a shriek and feel blood burst.

Blood's the best. Who cares where it comes from, how it gets on your lips an' hands. Blood is money is power is drugs. Blood's all I need. Violence is survival an' blood decides everything.

I'm in control.

"YA WEAK FUCKING FOOL YA PATHETIC WEAK BITCH YOU GONNA CRY GONNA FUCKING CRY YA…"

Been kicking his nose in forever when I see he's one o' mine.

All my boys are on the floor. Attackers, dealer, stash—long gone. Only bleeders on the scene; I'm embarrassed to call 'em mine.

Loyalty's a lie. Just means someone was too dumb to switch sides. No shame in might, right…

So maybe I was blinded by the thrill o' the fight, but what boy here could claim different. We're Hardihoods! We know the risk o' friendly fire. They know their king can get carried away, but the important thing's we were jumped and we're still standing, or at least I am, an' if I'm standing, so's everyone else, 'cause that's the point o' being The Head, that's the beauty o' *collective*. As long as the ones on top are alright, society'll be fine.

My boys gotta respect authority, even if I was letting off steam on the wrong face. There's no excuse for all of 'em to be out so easy. I need an army, not a pile o' rags!

"What the hell was that, boys?"

"You tell us," Cull moans through broken teeth. "You trying to teach us a lesson?"

I sneer.

"Whatever happened ta *manoeuvres*? Gotta be ready for anything! Can't trust no one, nothing, nowhere, never!"

Bic stands. His nose looks like it's sobbing cherries.

"We learned that alright."

So it's my fault? They'll leave this warehouse bruised but better for it. That's all they exist for, an' they know it.

Bic has his nose pushed on mine, so close he must be out of his tiny mind. Has he forgotten why we're here, what we came for, what we lost? All of 'em stink of mutiny.

This is the part thinkers dun' think of: the point where power may become a liability. 'Cept I got it on, 'cause I know how reality works, an' I can work it however I want.

"Don't blame me, boys! Blame the skeeze who jumped our deal!"

They break into laughs o' disbelief. My ears are hot enough to pop knuckles like sirens on silent.

Respect. Power. Control. Control's the utmost necessity. Have your head an' you have everyone else's. Handle your drink, drugs, women.

"Once in a while, some smart fuck will beat you to the punch. It's our job to hit back harder!"

"What are you on, man? Them's an idea! There was nothing but us in an empty warehouse and then you…!"

"You!" Cull snarls. "How dare you attack your own!"

I search for proof—bloody tracks of retreat, pocket knives dropped mid-fight, dust left behind from the biggest haul I've ever seen—an only find an echoing empty.

No rival gang. No pill. No deal.

Just us, an' me. I cornered the boys before they could think. Beat down kids dumb enough to call me a friend.

Kids dun' understand the food chain. Think you're on top means you've beaten the system? Hi-archy connects us. Leaders need followers an The Man needs boys to back 'im, otherwise he's just one freak with his whiskers twisted, slugging enemies only he can see.

"You need help, man," Bic puts his paw on me. "You need to see someone."

I shove him off. What's he thinking?

"Fuck this. I'm going back to my girl."

I swing my tail over my jacket—the Ramones patch I once chewed off a human's sleeve—an strut like any smart rat should, 'cause if you got your head on right, you got everything.

"That bitch better've left my meth alone."

SPEED TALKING

"Bitch snorted my meth. Bitch huffed up my fuckin' meth!"

Was that my boy? Yeah, he was right in front of me with his one bodyguard: the tall one missing his front teeth, allegedly the work of some sadistic human kid.

My boy looked ready to set hell on fire.

I couldn't care. I just wanted more speed.

He grabbed me by my ear. My tail twitched. Nose and whisks rat-a-tat-rattled. My fur buzzed like a bee's dick. The room seemed full of them with their angry, bloody eyes and pesticide squirting from their wings and I wanted more speed but knew it was all gone because I'd ripped apart his hole looking for it and there was no way I would've missed any and anyway why do they call it speed when it actually slows time down?

"Bitch! You hear me?"

Heard him, sure, but didn't really care to answer. For one thing there were all these bruises on my legs and I wondered where they came from and I knew what was coming and didn't plan on fighting but man sometimes you have to move and moving is the only thing you can do, even if moving means running right into a cat's paw, a dog's jaws, a nasty glue trap, because what the hell do we have brains for except bashing them in? Death probably takes longer than life, and man, I gotta keep moving, I gotta keep going, I gotta prove I'm alive.

He started ripping at my tail but I still felt all euphoric and edgy while he shook the whole world with his angry breath. I moved around a bit to make it harder for him, and he didn't like that one bit.

I felt nothing. Not even when he threw me over our couch—this cool Converse we nabbed off a human corpse.

My boy always got like this and I guess I can't blame him, I mean we all need somewhere to put our anger, so why not put it on me. I don't think it was his fault, really. Lots of the time he didn't know what he was doing. Or behaved the way he thought a bad boy like him has gotta be.

He wailed on me good. I stared at my legs. Where the hell did those bruises come from? They were such weird colours and seemed to move up and down my skin and sparkle like firecrackers and what if none of this was really happening? Human philosophy says nothing's real or something, so doesn't that mean you could do anything? Maybe I could wake up a pinky doe again with no bruises on my legs or speed in my brain and I'd be back home with my ten brothers and ten sisters and things could be okay.

Didn't happen. This was the only reality. The only one I was gonna get.

So I opened my eyes and looked my boy in the face. I stared so hard it scared him a sec. Have to admit, I didn't mind seeing him scared.

My nerves were still gone, asleep or on vacation. All the fear was gone too. My paranoia reached a whole new level, like I was on some higher frequency and no amount of blood could change that.

"You bitch! Want me to throw you in a trap?"

I was already in a trap. My whole life was a trap. My boy was my only chance at protection, but I really needed protection from him. He always said girls are easy to pick up and play with and throw out when the fun's over. Easy to slap around, too. What could I do? It's a big, bad world, man. Where could I go on my own? Where would I get my speed?

"You're still high right now, aren't you, slut? High on *my* drugs!"

When did I get on the floor? He kicked me again and again and there was this crazed squeak in my head and then I realized the squeaks were coming from me. Even his bodyguard was telling him to back off, but my boy was beyond listening to anybody.

He kicked me in that face he always called so pretty. He bashed in the brains he said I didn't have.

I heard a flick, saw a flash. His knife was out and almost on me, almost in me, and I was so numb at this point pain might have been okay.

It's stupid to jump someone who has a knife out.

I do lots of stupid things when I'm high.

I sunk my teeth in so deep I tasted bone. Now it was his turn to squeal and I grabbed the knife before it even hit the floor and knew exactly what to do with it.

Maybe if I'd gone to school, stayed clean, blown bucks on a useless arts degree, I would have ended up in a different reality, one that didn't hurt half as much.

I stabbed my boy a few times. Soon it didn't look like my boy anymore, just this furry mess of blood.

It wasn't too bad. He'd be okay the next day. And then I'd really be in for it!

Oh well. If this was my life, I might as well make the best of it. Every choice is a door, so why not walk through and see what happens?

He bubbled blood; I grabbed a handful of wood chips to munch. Maybe he'd be sorry after this, become a real gentleman, and we'd go off to live in a nest by the sea like he always promised, get off the drugs and have a litter or three.

Or maybe that was just the speed talking.

SUICIDE NOTE #3

It's moments like these I'm embarrassed by my preoccupation with material things. You truly can't take it with you. Perhaps you can't take anything. Which always leads me to wonder what the point is in the first place.

I am scared of dying. Well, I'm scared of doing it myself. I wouldn't say I fear death itself, but I fear opting out. What if it's wrong? What if it doesn't work? What if it does?

My suicide attempts/inclinations have always been a cry for help. Always. They're a signal I want a different life than the one I have rather than no life at all (Quoth my Jungian analyst).

The scary thing lately is that I can't imagine what could be different. Would I be less inclined to cut if I finally got my food processor? Would I forgo the urge to vomit if I finally got an agent/released a bestseller? Would any lover or cat or apartment, winterless city, steady income or community membership relieve me the inconvenience of this brain, perhaps this very spirit?

My Reiki practitioner told me one time that all she could hear during our treatment was, "This is a tortured spirit." But why?

Ugh. Whatever.

I'd like most everything donated. No funeral, please, and if there is one it better fucking not be in Deadton. Toast my memory in the Big City. Or Ireland. Somewhere that felt closer to home.

I'm not going to be all rash this time. I'm going to take things slow. I'll stick around, see if things improve. I'll give it 'til New Years.

2020's gonna bring in a whole new decade, a new time to flourish and grow. I trust that humankind will see better days, and I hope I will too, but it's wise to have a contingency plan for if your dreams fall through.

I don't want to die with bitterness in my heart but you fuckers really can go to hell. You know who you are. The ones who called me "slut" and "freak" and "emo" and "it" and whatever nasty label was in that season. Fuck you, enemies. Fuck you, so-called friends. Fuck you to every John who ripped me off and basically every boyfriend.

Maybe suicide is the preferred alternative to killing all you shits. That's really what I want, but I am impotent. And I'd rather not leave the world in a worse space than before I entered it. Even when people deserve to die, murder leaves a rift. Suicide is softer.

I really tried to make friends with the horrors in my head. I've tried affirmations and therapy and meditation and you know what, meditation worked, when I did it for three hours a day. I could cut, eat, starve, try to fuck the pain away. I can walk and write and smile at stars. I can smile at dogs and smile at babies and smile at lovers holding hands but that is not enough for one life to live on all alone.

I wanted to do good in the world. And I do want to die with hope. Hope for the future, gratitude for the past. I want to scream thank you to every sunset and rainbow and sunshower and storm and lake and ocean breeze I ever met. I want to thank the animals and the plants, the food, the hotel clerks and servers and cab drivers and guys who actually tipped. I want to thank you for believing in me even when I didn't deserve it.

I still believe we can do better than this. There are so many songs I wish I'd recorded, but my voice isn't good enough for them. I hope someone else will sing my songs for me.

Keep singing, sweet world. I will hear you and smile in my sleep.

Sorry I couldn't be there.

THIS HAPPENED #3
(BECHDEL TEST)

She wanted to meet me alone.

We chose the coffee shop on Knight and White.

She looked alright. Left Whatshisname a week ago and was already back to being human. But I knew it'd be a long road.

We chitted, chatted, shot shit. It was exactly what you'd expect from a coffee shop visit.

Then:

"Whatshisname bought me the nicest thing last week."

We'd danced around this all through our lattes.

"You're back with him?"

"Well…"

"Fuck sake." I snuck her muffin into my bag. "What do I always say?"

"Um, never trust a feminist?"

"Who wears red lipstick. That's a different thing. What do I always say about *men?*"

"Like literally nothing. Your entire life passes the Bechdel Test."

"What are you talking about? I have guy friends!"

"You do?"

"Never trust a man who likes dogs more than cats! Dogs can be trained. Cats can't."

"I know, I know. But he sounded so sincere on the phone," I knew that look: she was a lamb who thinks the slaughterhouse is a retirement home. "Maybe it'll be different this time."

***

She asked to meet me at the hospital.

If you've never been to a Big City infirmary, you're a lucky lady. Doctors are sent there for bad behaviour. People go to the ER to kill time.

She looked bad. Worse was the wear on the inside, that silent agony I'd witnessed so many times, on so many faces.

People don't believe me when I say whores are human, and the same goes for women. They have hearts, hopes, and heads, all too often stolen, dashed, cracked open. Equality didn't happen for everyone. Some of us are stuck, and we're all stuck with them.

I never know what to say. I like to think I float above the bullshit 'cause I like girls, but nobody's safe—certainly not from themselves.

I snuck a flower out of my bag.

She couldn't smile; it hurt.

"Whatshisname…"

"No." I touched her hand, then pulled away. "Let's not."

"Please. Your life may pass the Bechdel Test, but mine doesn't."

"Okay."

"Well, it was fine for a week. I really thought he'd changed. Then the mailman talked to me too long, and that was it.

I told him I couldn't take it anymore. I had to leave.

He said he couldn't let me."

This time, my hand stayed on hers.

"He thought he'd knocked me out. He must have, for a bit. I woke up next to a body bag. Heard him upstairs in the attic. The police found…something up there. I guess his plan was to cut me up so he could hide me more easily.

I got out. Crawled all the way to the neighbour's house. Don't remember much. The cops came. They got him. They really got him. For good this time."

***

Whatshisname had served five months when we met at the coffee shop again. She looked younger, freer, alive. Maybe she'd fallen in love; maybe she'd finally fallen in love with herself!

We gabbed, giggled, swapped war stories.

Then:

"Whatshisname called from prison."

"Shit. You didn't answer it?"

"Well…"

"No! C'mon! You can't get back with him! You can't!"

"I know, I know, it's just…" her eyes looked to something I couldn't see, "he sounded so sincere on the phone."

GET AWAY FROM
THAT CAR

I would have kissed the frost off the windshield. Couldn't reach. Too short. Too tired. In too much of a hurry.

They said you got away; you called shotgun, stole my shotgun, and ran.

They said you escaped the city.

No one ever escapes!

How could you leave without me?

We were meant to be together—maybe not forever, but for now.

Now is all I've ever known.

Bonnie might have made it without Clyde, but you wouldn't get far without me.

Everyone told you to dump me: the lez girls, the straight guys, the ones who couldn't make up their mind. Everyone hated me.

I said I didn't care.

I did.

You may think I'm this hot mess devoid of responsibility, but I know regret, and I know your smiles mean you want to cry.

I know you're a criminal, but who cares? So am I.

I never meant to lead you on. I can't be monogamous, but I am ardent, and all my love's for you. This is a fidelity only crazy can cultivate—the kind that makes me chase you across countries.

I wore the dress you hated: the one made of cellophane, with the leopard panties underneath. I looked like a rock ready to roll. I looked so scary it was sexy.

Everyone says they hate the Big City, but how can anyone hate home? Whether you like it or not, home's where you come from, and where you come from is where you belong. Maybe the city got us all stuck 'cause it couldn't stand to let us go.

Because it loved us too much.

I thought I'd be the first to leave. I thought you'd be the one chasing after me. I'm not the one who gets left! I'm the one that gets to go; I'm the one who *gets it*. These are the affirmations I repeat every morning, even though they're not true (yet).

So far, reality sucks.

We do what we must to get better.

I freshened up the lipstick you said was too red. Fixed the mirrors, straightened the seat, pushed him out by way of my glittery platform boots, him splattering out the passenger door onto the tarnished macadam. Blood bubbled from his lips.

You may have taken my gun, but the truth is, I never needed it.

I can kill with a glance.

I would have kissed the frost off the windshield, but maybe it was clear the whole time. Maybe winter had long melted away, and for the first time, I'd end up where I wanted to be.

THE BALLAD OF ICARUS

—an excerpt

I don't know who's worth saving.

Someone smells like you. Someone asks, "Are you having fun, Kitty?" and I think I am.

Almost everyone can hear music, but not everyone can feel it.

To be the centre of all things you must also be on the periphery.

Exhibit A: I don't know anyone here. The only reason I was invited to the launch of a VR Arcade is because the Event Coordinator happens to be one of my only Facebook friends in The Big City. I probably couldn't recognize her in public, and it turns out I don't, because three hours in, I realise she's the tall grown-up in the strappy red dress.

Wasn't she two years younger than me? Did she grow up while I gave in? Am I staying free while she's locked in?

Exhibit B: I am intruding on their date. They* got dressed up and everything. I asked if it was okay if I tagged along for the ride since I was thinking of going anyway, and I've allowed them every possible private moment, which is easy for me, because I am weirdly happy alone—at least for a moment.

*They are Rain** and Zahi.

**Rain is Zahi's latest distraction from Abena.

Nobody's dancing except me. We all find our own ways to have fun. Most everyone is in virtual reality, but I would rather be here.

One of the volunteers shows me his own project: a meditation session with acid visuals. I dig it. I'm glad people want to bring consciousness along to the virtual realm. He asks if I want to plug in to one of the games and I say, "I'm okay. I did VR once. Don't feel the need to do it again. Like cocaine."

He is amazed.

Just like those guys are amazed when they see me whip out my flip phone by the coats. They hold it in their palms like a precious, ancient relic.

I ask them if my acid has melted on my tongue yet (Zahi gave me a quarter tab on the dance floor).

Meanwhile, on the dance floor, I groove with the Asian guy but don't have time to get his number.

"I hope you will forgive me if I don't indulge the societal propriety of a seatbelt,"—this is after the acid was about to kick, after Z&R wanted to head back to get ready for the next level of their journey to which I may or may not be invited (and assume I am not, for emotional safety's sake), when I could have stayed longer to dance harder.

One of the best things you can learn is when it's a good time to leave.

They use Good and Bad to push us down, but that doesn't negate the possibility of an objective or universal good—does it?

We discuss this intensely for about five minutes (by "we" I mean, me and Zahi), but there's really not much more to comment on except should I or should I not candy flip? Is it okay if I tag along on the tail of the milky way? If it's all going to Hell anyway, can I leave a kiss on your brain? It doesn't have to be sexy. I just want you to know I care. I mean if you want sex I'm (possibly) game but I'd rather...

Lots of people are lonely and alone. A guy literally said meeting me made his life better just because I hope he has a good day.

I am not a fucking saviour. I tried the hero thing, and you heard it here first:

Heroes don't work.

I envy their life together. The seeming simplicity of their kisses.

"Don't kiss me, do your drugs," Rain says.

All I hear is drugs, drugs, drugs. I'm getting the punch line without the joke. Story of my life. They are wondering whether they are good bad adults or bad good adults. They talk about how their bosses actually care about them but they're so scared of changing jobs and when I ask them why, they don't want to talk about it. They'd rather discuss drugs.

Specialness can be frightening, but there's never a reason to be afraid.

Listening to Alan Watts and Busy Signal may be the perfect concoction for my first acid trip.

You can structure the creative process, but can't force it. Like life, the best parts *happen*, and you cannot plan, contain or define them. They simply are and will be exactly as they are and always will be and they will kiss on the couch and there will be beauty in your periphery and you will be alone and it may actually be okay.

It may not be okay. Being alone may suck even on the good days. Then again that's a limited perspective for they sent us to live life and they certainly didn't mean for us to do it on our own, but we have to be alone for the better parts of the day, and anyway, it's all beautiful so why not live this? Why not take a sip of his mushroom smoothie which happens to taste like strawberry heaven? Why not laser flip? (Mushrooms + acid.) Or Jedi flip, for fun? (M added to the mix.) Why not love everything? Everything could become loveable the moment you decide to love it.

I would love to write a book that everyone could love. It's impossible, but—

If everyone loved. If everyone really, truly loved.

Love. What a childish attempt to encapsulate the better parts of the universe. The only part that's real, the only part that lasts.

We don't have to call it God. Maybe God is dead because people don't want that word anymore and if God has to die for a better world then She will, again and again and again.

I am not the saviour. I'm the crucifix. We are the cross you were laid upon. We are the prison to which you were condemned. The fire on which you were thrown.

I will keep trying harder, I promise, I am sorry, I fucked up, sometimes I suck at this, sometimes we all suck—

And that's okay.

I believe in life because they laugh, because they kiss and laugh and love and get all fucked up on the couch. I feel how I felt at my sister's wedding, like I am allowed to believe in love, even love in that lame-ass reductive sense, and she says, "interesting, bottles of colourful," and I guess we have to skip to The End when I peaked listening to *212* because who the fuck wouldn't?

Then Cakes Da Killa, *Keep It Goin*. I feel like my ribs have busted and it's very, very good.

It just so happened that Cakes Da Killa was the next person to play on Spotify after I begged Zain to play *212* by Azaelia Banks because there was nothing else I could listen to in that moment.

Modern Shakespeares realised genius is better to a beat. Saul Williams is certainly in on it. I'm sure many many many many many many more understand and will seek to be understood, if we can, Yes we can, I will try, I will, I am.

In other news, I *Lost My Mind* to Elley Duhe and they talked and I forgot everything that mattered. "I could get better one day at a time." That's what Elley told me through the speakers.

I decide it's okay to be scared. We are all insecure. To really be with people I have to be exactly as I am. I must give myself permission to exist. I will be real and afraid with them, because in the end, they are not afraid, they have already been to the other side, if there is one, and they seem to think it's all okay so what's the trouble, really?

On the free Spotify app you can skip ahead, but can't go back. Guess that forces us not to dwell on the past. Which is a good thing—right?

The trouble is, I want to relive the shit that makes me uncomfortable. Isn't that how we learn from it? Isn't that why I ruminate? Isn't that why I'm paranoid, with or without acid?

I want to do better. I want to be forgiven. I want to say sorry if that's what it takes and if it's better to forget for your sake then I will.

It's like being alone. If they have to be this high in a crowded room with a lot of people and even more music, I get that, I respect it. I am okay with being here alone and high if I have to be.

Of course, I could go to the club with them. Elbow-up in dopamine and licking up my madness.

I get lost in the lush snow. It is so pretty and perfect in this first descent and Zahi asks if I'm good but only for a second because he already knows the answer.

Am I good? Are you kidding me? This is the start of my life!

I can't get through the door. The bouncers peg me right away and I have to throw out my water bottle (Zahi got in with his). By this point I still feel like things could be chill, but then we are diverted from the dance floor by the coat check.

Now here I am slipping through the cracks of human consciousness, the space of human bodies, the promise of dance.

I am sure I dance for an hour or so but as we know music hits me hard enough sober; throw in a light show…

Brain opens and explodes. Hell is everywhere and real. Such easy little words to say but of course the weight is enough for Atlas to shrug it all off all over again. I have to keep taking breaks for water and eventually all I can do is pump my hips to the bass.

A girl crouches down with me and asks if I need a chair when I'm on the floor texting a wonderland message to the universe.

A girl shoves me to the centre of the dance floor when I'm on the edge of the heat.

A girl gets excited about my tattoo, takes me to the bathroom to show me hers, then seems embarrassed and puts all her walls way back up when I ask if she wants to go outside. I know then it's time to go, because any longer and I won't even know how to get my coat back, so I do, and the coat girl's nice and tells me to have a great night.

Zahi and Rain said they would protect me. Zahi and Rain said I had to stay with them the whole time.

Fuck them. They don't care about me anyway.

I'm off into the snow to contemplate loneliness, homelessness, dehydration, death, and oh the cold is a bone and my heart is the saw.

I left my keys behind—purposefully, because Zahi had his, and roommates who trip together stay together, but that's not how real life is.

I take what feels like the slowest walk in the world back to our place (but really, it's his).

I remind myself at worst it will only be an hour, and then the bar will have to close.

Panic. Grips me. Will the terror always be there? Will I ever let (it) go? Will I ever forgive myself not being strong enough to deal with everyone else's shit 360 days a year?

Three young, white people let me in to the building (I assume because I too am young and white). The boy says to me, so sweetly, "Cold night out there tonight, isn't it?" and I remember the kindness of strangers, and know I am soon going to be safe and home where I can write the shit out of the world.

Eventually they come home, and those who promised to be my side ditch me for the comfort of a bed and relationship.

I want to be okay with this. I want to love being alone. But without someone to love, nowhere feels like home.

I want to embrace the discomfort. I want to shed light on all things. I want you to see this/me: the love and terror that grips me daily. I want to see who you are. I want your small town heritage high class spoiled bitch colour blind ignorant fat ass anti-age acne scar second-gen awkward burnout bullshit. I see it all and I tell you, *You Are Beautiful, Dammit!*

The workout videos mean it when they say Step Out Of Your Comfort Zone.

Life is exactly what they taught you to be afraid of.

The best life is on the other side of risk.

So be afraid. Push past the fear. Then you will begin to live, and I promise it will be worth it.

Everywhere can be where you go to be yourself. Your life is a dance floor and you are always centre stage, so dance however you want.

Whatever you do, do you, and do so with love.

It's love that matters, not happiness. If you're always worried about being happy, you'll always be one step behind yourself. When you surrender to love—and that's what it is, surrender—you open up to the harsh painful blissful perfect reality of the Now, where so much is broken and all is solved.

I so feared the world would break me, or that I might break the world.

Why did I think that mattered? Humans have been addicted to trauma and drama for centuries. Maybe forever.

It's like when the Eurthymics came on and we all know that song and I said, "This song has some terrible messages about love," but while I was dancing I realised it was about sex, which of course, for me, is the same thing.

"Some of them want to use you, some of them want to get used by you; Some of them want to abuse you; some of them want to be abused."

Then I think of Sophia in Shortbus bitching at Sevryn about how romance, sex, and life are not black and white, impossible to reduce to dom or sub.

There is more than eat or be eaten. There is more than leave or be left. We can all stick together, we can do it alone, we can get through this. You can, you will.

I am. I did.

There will be scary, lonely nights, whether you're having a breakdown or living outside (or both), whether you failed miserably or your mom just died, and nothing will ever make that alright, but you will get through. Love is always on the other side.

Love is on the other side of everything.

Love is on the other side of risk.

If there's one thing I could ask it would be please don't protect us. Let me live, let me try, please be there when I fall, but please let me jump on my own because who knows

I just might fly this time.

VIBRATIONIS VIBRISSAE

Helioplex Aster Ism 2.6598 (Aster to his friends, though Techopods don't have "friends" as much as "familiar entities with mutually beneficial objectives") was summoned to the denarena for his data delineation.

"Helioplex Aster Ism. All the best to your data."

"And all the best to yours," Aster noted his Superior's speech. "Clarification required. Are you utilizing…?"

"The homo sapien communication system known as 'English.' Correct. Determined advisable to align translators on transport system for purposes of your advance acclimation."

"Confirmed."

Techopods don't bother with frivolous aesthetics like windows. Their transport systems, or "spaceships" as they might be considered by Earthly readers, moved from math alone. Therefore, Aster was spared the eerily poignant blue-and-green surface of his planetary target.

"Repeat primary objective."

"Infiltrate the bipedal race of homo sapiens known as humans on the ellipsoid Tellerium .87x, known to its inhabits as Earth."

"Repeat means of enaction."

"Take on the form of a bipedal homo sapien to ascend social hierarchy."

"Repeat ultimate objective."

"Kill all the cats."

"Describe target item 'cat.'"

"Cat. Felis catus. Small to mid-size mammalian, carnivorous quadruped, domesticated by the homo sapiens."

"Clarify necessity for extermination."

"The cat emits a tonal fluttering, vibrationis vibrissae, called "purrs" by the humans. These "purrs" emit a frequency into all adjacent universes compelling all conscious and unconscious beings to experience tissue regeneration (if they have tissue), reduction in blood pressure (if they have blood), and, worst of all, intense feelings of harmony, pleasure, and love. Techopods must destroy love and anything that incites love across all universes."

"Confirmed, Helioplex A. Summarize data-gathering."

"I have data-gathered on humans extensively. I know exactly how to imitate their behaviour and dialect as found at our geographical touchpoint. I have practiced cultivating what humans call "charisma", a social and psychological quality that inspires admiration, devotion, and, when properly enacted, complacency. I will convince the humans to kill all the cats whilst barely lifting a jointed digit, or, as the humans say, finger."

"No distractions. Cats necessitate extermination. May your data go with you."

"May your data go with you."

As Aster hovered above the drop-pod, his Superior warned him, "Recall, Helioplex. Tellerium atmosphere warps our communication systems. Store cranial activity to data log. Contact will be made when open channels available. Otherwise, you go, and you go alone."

"I shan't fail, Superior. The cats are as good as gone."

The Superior signaled Aster to drop out into the ozone. He couldn't help but feel (feel? was he human already?) his Superior was ushering him into— what did humans call it?

Ah, yes: Hell.

***

Objective:

   Take human form.

   Kill all the cats.

Aster's body fused into its protective shell to withstand the heat and pressure of entering a foreign ozone layer. The Superior's calculations were precise and Aster descended at an exact angle and velocity to facilitate material transmutation.

Techopods have no use for magic, but their transmutation resembles it. They need only correctly implement the data of one specific form, often followed by one specific action item, and they will land on a new, vulnerable planet ready to data-gather (and destroy any active love outputs).

Earth's ozone hit Aster like a tidal wave of flaming bricks.

The ozone was supposed to be thinner than this.

Aster only ever trusted data.

Now, data failed him.

His computations were scrambled in the heat.

He tried to focus, but Earth wasn't letting that happen.

Objective:

   Take

177

all the cats

Kill

human form

Object

the

kill

Ivethetakecatsformhumanobjective

Take

cats

Kill

form

all the

cats

take   form

the all objective kill

human

take   form

cat

Heat, then cold.

Light, then darkness.

***

Helioplex A. data log 1.1

Crash-landing on flat geographic region covered in the aesthetically-pleasing vegetation humans call "grass." Saturated verdant hue/soft texture. Incorrectly presumed to be preferred surface for human transportation (the farther into populated areas one traverses, the less grass one sees).

Primary heat/light source ("the sun") appears as aureate sphere in upper atmosphere. Air heavily oxygenated.

I was expecting more dexterity from my upper limbs, on which humans tend to be reliant, but have not found success so far. Indeed, I have had to crawl on all fours to my first destination, assumably a side-effect from the crash, one that should quickly abate.

Other noted sensory changes: hearing much improved, seemingly above the average sonar rate of humankind, with eyesight adapted to motion and detecting close range objects. Another side effect (presumed).

Will update when human contact is made.

DATA LOG 1.1 COMPLETE—SENT

***

Imogen walked the Big City streets wondering if people could ever change.

Perhaps the real question was: could they change for the better?

Imogen was different since art school. Her hair was shorter (to match her life span), her pant size bigger (to match her debt). What remained constant was her relentless pursuit of self-destruction, despite all her attempts to be what she called "a decent human."

Why was she the only one exempt from her own compassion?

Like with work. Why didn't she apply for that arts curator job? She fit the educational requirements. What stopped her? How was it better for her career to stay working at Paints 'n Stuff?

Or romance. Why didn't she ask out that nice girl who went on and on about Eva Gonzales? Why did she go for guys who said they were artists but were really alcoholics who liked having an excuse for hitting on models, who didn't even want to argue impressionism vs expressionism, and never wanted to play with natural light, unless it was in your bedroom.

Had Imogen walked down Dun or King, her life may have continued as normal. Instead, she turned the corner on Hope, and saw the last thing she would have expected.

***

Helioplex A. data log 1.2

Situation urgent.

First human contact made:

  Subject: Female. Mid-to-low socio-economic status. Posturing: Friendly.

Subject and I sighted each other concomitantly. Immediately noted substantial height and size differential. Also noted female's use of extremely high vocal register when addressing me. Concern expressed for damage incurred by narrow escape from a motor vehicle humans use for expedited transport (said encounter resulted in my inability to resist female's approach). Female lifted me into her own motor vehicle (again, larger than anticipated). Motor vehicle included reflective surfaces enabling first sighting of personal physical form since crash.

Visual report:

  Two large eye sockets with pale yellow irises and dilated almond pupils. Canine teeth protruding from mouth. Evident vibrissae alongside either cheek. Stripe-patterned titian fur. Straight flare-based ears, triangle shaped, close-set on top of head.

Evidently, transmutation objective scrambled owing to miscalculations regarding Tellerium ozone density.

I am a cat.

Um, Data Log? Cancel recording. Send report as incomplete.

DATA LOG 1.2 INCOMPLETE—SENT

I'm humiliated. (That's the term humans use to describe the emotional strain onset by one's personal failures/inadequacies.)

The self-appointed human caregiver (called "Imogen") put me in a ventilated carrier for transport to a veterinarian clinic. Second human contact made in the form of an animal medical examiner who was concerned by my "unnatural gait" (I have yet to perfect navigation on all fours). The close encounter with a transport vehicle left no permanent material errors: paw is bandaged, and due to heal.

Imogen has placed a small polyester strap around my neck, presumably for identification purposes.

She calls me "Alistair."

Imogen is surprisingly docile, far unlike humans as portrayed in Tellerium history.

She is what humans describe as "affectionate." To myself, and other humans, though evidently her higher pitch is reserved for me.

Situation remains stable, albeit limiting. Sustenance, hydration, and shelter are all provided by Imogen without any apparent interest in personal gain— motive? Clarification required.

Current action item:

  Enact global feline genocide.

How to complete said task when I myself am a cat?

Imogen's lower socio-economic status is confirmed by the low square footage of her residence. Appears to derive pleasure or purpose (or both) from spreading a coloured, slightly viscous, wet substance over blank surfaces to form abstract images (my data-logues confirm high likelihood of her being an "artist").

She talks to me like I can understand.

Unbeknownst to her, I can.

"Some people say rescue cats are difficult, but I disagree. Know why, Alistair? All you need to do is respect their boundaries. Like people."

Boundaries. Unfamiliar concept. Techopods only care about data, no matter how we get it. The concept that some data may be best left alone is…intriguing.

Humans sleep at night, when the sun sets out of the sky and the moon rises and reflects its illumination. Do cats sleep at night? Must confirm.

For now, I watch Imogen drool on a pile of drawings.

She helped me fix my paw.

She helped me.

I am suddenly grateful I have not been sent here to exterminate humans, for this particular specimen may have complicated things.

It is clear that humans are not so void of love as Techopods were led to believe.

This is a secret I am currently willing to keep.

***

Third human contact made.

Subject: Male. Mid-to-high socio-economic status. Posturing: Hostile.

"Alistair? Alistair! Meet a new friend! This is Carter."

"Nice place. I usually don't come down this far south. Too many criminals—if you know what I mean. But no, I mean, it's a nice place, real nice."

"Uh… thanks?"

Carter grabs Imogen and puts his mouth on hers. They are kissing. I do not like it. Not that it matters. I need to find cats and start killing them. Perhaps these humans will be of use to me. I must simply maintain maximum cerebral engagement…

"Hey, little buddy."

NO TOUCH BELLY!

"Shit!" the male called "Carter" jumps back. "That cat is crazy!"

"He's a rescue," Imogen sounds like she's apologizing for me. Unappreciated. "Let him come to you."

"Fat chance."

"I thought you liked cats!"

"Oh, yeah, of course I do!"

"Well, then…"

"Shit! Did you see that?"

"What?"

"The cat was walking on its hind legs!"

Behaviour deemed suspicious. Must persist to walk four-legged until discomfort ebbs. More data required.

Carter repeats invasion of personal space. What was that phrase Imogen used? Ah, yes: he doesn't respect boundaries.

"Is he…glaring at me?"

"Cats don't glare, Carter."

"Seriously, Imogen, that's the weirdest cat I've ever seen."

I've aroused suspicion. Carter is a threat.

Impetus to data-gather.

***

Imogen is away for the night, presumed to be at Carter's residence.

That is fine. That is good. I am pleased, not perturbed, no, to be perturbed would imply I appreciate her company and I do not, no—I miss the scratches, that's all.

This gives me opportunity to collect data on

A) cat behaviours

B) means of escape from human abodes

C) means of effectively disposing of cats (while also being a cat)

Imogen has several material data logs ("books") about cats. I lack the required strength to pick up a book and open it, but have discovered cats are very good at knocking things over.

***

Paw manipulation improved. Turning pages successful. Useful data collected.

Cats do:

> Purr when contented
>
> Hiss when agitated
>
> Flick tail when energized/agitated
>
> Spit when aggressive
>
> Sit on human laps, when inclined
>
> Receive "pets" from humans, when inclined
>
> Use human waste disposal methods as provided by humans by way of "litter boxes"

"Groom" by way of licking their fur/paws/privates

"Play" (must explore further)

Cats do not:

attempt human speech (MUST REFRAIN)

use human waste disposal methods (unless trained)

walk on hind legs (MUST REFRAIN)

narrow their eyes/glare when displeased (MUST REFRAIN)

It's increasingly ironic that I gathered extensive intel on human behaviour, yet failed to thoroughly educate myself on the targets of extermination. I merely assumed ingratiating myself with the humans was the primary objective. Humans en masse have been convinced time and time again to destroy nature, wildlife (often to extinction), and even other groups of humans (sometimes also to extinction).

Humans are destructive. I long ago concluded this. I must merely extract this tendency for my own means.

If only I could talk without arousing suspicion!

***

Imogen knew she'd made a mistake.

Carter was just another jerk in sheep's clothing.

Why did she keep looking for love in all the wrong places, or looking for love at all?

What kept her complacent? Sex? The illusion of security?

Maybe it was an excuse to never grow.

If she was always with the same type of person, she was always stuck in the same place, and even though she was miserable, she was safe.

185

"What do you think, Alistair?" Imogen rubbed her rescue cat's ear. "Is change worth it? Is change even possible?"

***

I'm enjoying a sunbath at Imogen's feet while she paints.

HELIOPLEX A. DO YOU READ ME?

Sigh. Yes. You don't have to beam at me so loud.

REGRET. THIS IS A TENUOUS FREQUENCY. SITUATION URGENT.

You don't say.

RECEIVED DATA THAT YOUR OBJECTIVE WAVES WERE SCRAMBLED AND YOU HAVE ACTUALLY

You don't have to shout—

TURNED INTO A CAT.

Ah. Yeah.

SINCE THEN WE HAVE NOT RECEIVED ANY DATA LOGS. UPDATE REQUIRED.

No update yet. Still a cat.

CAN YOU ALTER MATERIAL FORM?

Negative. Multiple attempts/failures.

REGRET.

Will continue mission in current form.

SITUATION URGENT. FELINE CRANIAL CAPACITY LIMITED.

PLEASE. STOP. SHOUTING.

Proper attenuation of volume?

Confirmed.

The longer you remain a cat, the less likely you will be able to retain and therefore complete your mission objective.

Meaning?

A cat can only be a cat.

Faulty conclusion. Cats often fight other cats. Mission remains tenable.

NEGATIVE.

Attenuate volume!

Corrected. Working on equation to safely carry you out of ozone whereby you will be quarantined and dematerialized if feline form proves irreversible.

CLARIFICATION REQUIRED!!!

Attenuate volume. New objective: Remove self from human vicinity. Remain still to ensure maximum teleportation efficiency. Wait-time approx 20= to 2)00 megaparcs.

HISS.

Clarification required?

Um. Auditory anomaly. Will update.

***

I must finalize my plans for world domination!

First, I must groom. Sensation is satisfying, as are the results.

It's correct that my current feline form causes difficulty. Imogen is a benevolent "momma," but does not let me outside. Any chance of escape by way of the front door is thwarted by her judiciousness. I must admit, she's admirable.

Distractions need to be avoided. My subjective consciousness is at stake. I must strategize!

After some scratches.

Now. 20= megaparcs is almost 1 turn around the sun on Earth, giving me ample time to ascend to my rightful role as feline dictator, thus fulfilling my objective to destroy all cats in existence, except me, as my existence as a feline is inconsequential, because, as Carter likes to constantly remind my momma (that is, Imogen), I do not purr.

He also likes to remind her of his dominance over her, which I detest, not because I can spare any affection for her, no, not at all, I have no room for compassion whilst I plot genocide, I merely am affronted by his ignorance as I am obviously superior to them both.

Cats may already rule this world. Humans do everything for us (or, them). People love cats, as a rule, and as for the ones who don't...

"FUCKING PIECE OF SHIT!"

"Leave him alone!"

"Look at these scratches! He attacked me!"

"And what did you do to provoke him?"

"You care more about that dumb cat than me!"

"You don't need protecting! He does!"

Carter exits abruptly, and not without rage.

Pleased.

***

Dum de dum dum...

I am learning to "play!"

Imogen has provided me with several items of amusement, including but not limited to a contraption that chirps when I bite it, and seemingly possesses a substance of the psychoactive variety. Enjoyable. Must explore further.

I appreciate these teeth. And the paws! I initially deemed human hands superior, but human hands cannot utilize scratch posts to the same satisfaction.

CANNOT...REACH...

Oh, shit. They found me.

TO…TELEPORT…

DNA…FREQUENCY…

NO…LONGER…MATCHING…

! Oh…

PROVIDE…GEOGRAPHIC…COORDINATES…

Nah.

CLARIFI…CATION…RE…QUIRED…

Cats don't like being told what to do.

TRANSMISSION…FAILING>>>>>>>>>>

Byyyye!

***

Wake up. Stretch. Momma?

MEOW!

"I'm here, cutie. Want some pumpkin?"

Mmm.

"Carter called today."

Hiss.

"You really don't like him, do you?"

Doesn't respect boundaries.

"Hmm. Well, anyway. He bought a cat! Trying to prove himself, I guess.
Says we could both come over and meet it. Are you going to be nice?"

Reowr?

"To him, and to the cat."

…Cat?

Objective…

Object…

Cat…

Sounds…

Familiar…

"Give us a kiss?"

Yuss!

***

Momma puts me in carrier. Hiss.

Momma gives treats. Better.

Stupid Carter. Hiss.

They let me out. Stretch. Sniff.

Smells like…

"Alistair, meet Morrigan!"

Black furry paws whiskers…

Cat?

CAT!!

***

Imogen wrangled Alistair into his carrier while Morrigan shot around like a rocket in abject distress.

"SEE? I knew this was a bad idea! He's the sweetest bean alone, but any time he sees another cat, it's like he wants to kill it!"

"You care about that stupid cat more than me!"

"And you don't care about anyone but yourself!"

"Wait, the door! SHIT! You bitch! That dumb thing cost me 100 bucks!"

"I can't blame your cat for running away! We're all better off without you!"

Imogen never slammed a door before. It felt good.

Imogen saved Alistair (formerly Helioplex Aster Ism 2.6598), but as it turned out, Alistair saved her, too.

People could change. Aliens, too.

Was it for the better?

Maybe, maybe not.

What did it matter, in the long run?

***

Momma takes me home.

Food. Lick. Curl. Sleep.

Momma's lap. Warm. Pets.

Purr!

ADAM'S APPLES

Once upon an apocalypse, in an abandoned high-rise apartment, the last two businessmen on earth were having an argument.

In better days, they had tailored suits, shined shoes, styled hair, and manicured nails. Now their suits were wrinkled, their shoes sullied, their hair/nails unkempt, what with being unable to access a tailor, shoe-shiner or barber, what with being unable to walk the street without encountering armageddon.

The short, dark one (Jude) tried to help the tall, blonde one (Chris) look on the bright side.

"Coreless apples, Chris! We invented coreless apples! We basically saved the world!"

"No, we destroyed the world, remember?" Chris countered. "Our genetically modified spores leaked into the troposphere, infecting the global community with Apathy."

"Yeah, yeah…"

Chris stared out the window. Fires raged in the West, floods rose in the East, ice stormed the South, and to the North, things looked okay.

"Everyone got fat, sick, stopped shaving in the shower, stopped shaving, stopped showering! The ocean levels rose, nobody cared. Poverty gaps widened, nobody cared! Now we're the last people on earth!"

Jude protested,

"We may not be the last…"

"Well," Chris pressed his head on the glass, "we're the last ones who care! Nobody else cared enough to take the vaccine."

"Lot of good it's done us! We're just gonna die, like everybody."

Jude avoided looking out the windows. The world was redolent of a violent video game with the unappreciated addition of smells.

"Remember the girl?"

"I remember, Chris."

"I can still see her!"

"I said I remember!"

"We tried to take her with us, but she wouldn't leave the couch! Then when we grabbed her, dropped her, and accidentally smashed her head through the television set, all she said was, "There goes my TV.""

"Not the best last words ever spoken," Jude agreed.

"Remember those teenagers watching the police shoot each other? They just sat there, munching popcorn."

"They probably thought it was VR. Now stop it! You're making me crave popcorn."

"We're going to die, aren't we?"

"Everyone dies! What matters is how long you fight it!"

Chris was too busy pontificating to fight anything.

"There must be more to life than death! I remember when people started to not care. Imagination became a novelty, sex a chore. I tried to remind people of the joy in seeing a baby smile or the sun rise."

"You did not!"

"Well, I thought about it! I was just busy. Trying to cover up the apple problem."

"Quit acting like it's all our fault! The phones didn't help much either."

Chris relented, "True. Particularly after the cerebral wi-fi implantations. And what did the government do, hmm? Nothing! They didn't care!"

"To be fair, they stopped caring long before the Apathy struck."

"They're probably in their bunkers sipping champagne as we speak."

"What kind of champagne?"

"Probably a—it doesn't matter!"

Jude sighed, "I'd love a drink!"

"There's no time for drinking! We have to save the world!"

"It's a little late." Jude toed a garbage pile that might have once been laundry, "If only we had an Xbox…"

"There's more than video games at stake! It's our task to preserve humanity! To risk everything and start anew! To rekindle whatever hope lies dormant in the hearts of men!"

"But we're the only men left!"

"Well…" Chris struggled, "There could be women out there. Or some genderfluid folks…"

Outside, the fires and floods duked it out. It was like TV, but louder.

The worst part about the end of the world was Chris and Jude were misfits. Two exclamation points in a world full of ellipses. Too much feeling, too many inflections. They alone would suffer, for they alone cared.

Jude reclined on the couch the previous residents allowed to dust, then rot. He gazed at his friend with something like sympathy.

"I'm sorry you're so bummed over the end of the world!"

Chris tore his eyes from the calamity.

"We shouldn't argue. Love is the only thing that will keep us together! Like Lincoln said, A house divided cannot stand!"

"Who?"

"What do you mean, who?!"

"I dunno. I feel like I could remember…" Jude curled up on the arm rest, "but who cares?"

Chris' panic reached a peak freak.

"Not you too! Didn't you take the vaccine when I did?"

"I was going to, but we were so busy trying to cover up the apple thing…then I thought I was immune…eh, who cares…"

Chris lifted his friend by the collar and gave him a good shake.

"C'mon! Snap out of it!"

To no avail: Jude yawned while Chris cried the last tears on earth.

"What will it take to make you care?"

Chris dropped Jude; from his new vantage point on the floor, Jude noticed something on the coffee table.

"Huh. These guys left some weed…"

He proceeded to roll a half-assed joint. Chris continued his meltdown.

"What makes people care?! Dammit! I knew we shouldn't have used the Tao Te Ching as toilet paper! Now I'm going to die, and you won't even keep me company in my misery!"

"We all die. You don't seem to get that…"

Chris moaned.

"Why you worrying, man?" Jude licked the paper. "What if Apathy isn't the disease? What if it's the cure?"

Outside, the floods won: water pushed on the windows. The glass creaked;

the panes squeaked.

"What do you want to do?" Jude asked, but didn't really care.

Chris sat. His eyes flickered with something like emotion—then it was gone.

"Pass the joint, I guess."

BUDDHAFIELD

It was the perfect day.

Abel woke to butterflies thrumming outside his window. They were yellow, and caught the light.

Were they playing, making love, or both?

The boy stretched in his silk sheets. He was young. He was healthy.

Was he free?

This last wondering, which woke him daily, remained unanswered by his tutors or his Father.

Yet, his Father loved him, as did his tutors.

What was freedom compared to love?

***

Abel's Father was mostly comprised of computers. He had a chin, and a beard that went down to his toes, and his toes were so long he couldn't have stood even if he'd had legs. He was wired up, held down, plugged in so he could see, speak, think, and feel.

He could have built himself a body, but as he told Abel, he was tired of walking around.

Abel sat with his Father every morning for breakfast. Abel ate berries; his Father derived alimentation from the monitors.

"How did you sleep, my son?" Father's chin stood still, but Abel could hear him.

"Well, Father. And you? Good dreams?"

They laughed. Father's computers could do many things, but had yet to learn how to dream.

***

The grass was green; the air was clean; the sky was red.

Abel attended his studies morning until evening: History, Sciences, Hygiene, Music, and Pleasures. He pet lions in the menagerie. He splashed in the outdoor pools.

Every day was the same, until the day it wasn't.

Abel's tutors loved him; he didn't return the favour. All except one. He was younger than the others, with brown skin three shades darker than Abel's, and coiled black hair. He let Abel ask questions, and more importantly, answered them.

One day, his beloved tutor had a cough.

The next day, he was gone.

Nobody told him where his favourite teacher went, and he knew better than to ask.

Besides, there were other distractions.

Father wanted to prepare him for adulthood, and sent a priestess to teach him the ways of love. Abel knew she was beautiful, but was more interested in the ground's green trees and the sky's pink clouds, or finding out where his tutor went.

She took him to a secret place where they would share the sacred embrace, but instead of kissing him, she whispered in his ear,

"Do you want to know the truth?"

Truth troubled him; he sensed much was omitted in his lessons. But what was truth compared to love?

Her next whisper made the sky turn blue.

"Don't you want to know about your brother?"

***

She told him what to do.

"You must pierce the walls of the world, and enter the unknown."

She told him how to do it.

"You must climb the tallest limb of the highest tree and touch the largest fruit."

She didn't tell him what to expect.

Yet, how could he not move forward, now that he knew there was somewhere to go?

There was a brother he had never known, who could yet be found.

The highest tree was in the centre of Father's kingdom. Abel had scarcely noticed it before. Now it was his brightest beacon—and darkest omen.

There comes a time in everyone's life that they must do what they must.

This was Abel's moment.

He touched the trunk. Though his Father was back home, Abel worried he already knew what his son was about to do.

The boy rested a foot on the lowest branch.

Nothing.

The trunk abetted his ascension.

Silence.

He reached for the higher branches…

BEEP.

"Warning. Security level breached."

What if someone saw him? What if he pushed himself off the edge of the world? What waited outside perfection?

He had to know. He had to keep climbing.

"Warning. Warning. Warning."

BEEP. BEEP. BEEP.

He aimed for the biggest, brightest fruit, and plucked it, but it remained on the branch.

Above, a door opened.

He was beyond.

He was free.

***

Father built the world from chaos. That was what Abel was taught every day in History.

And lo, Mars was Nothing, and Father brought it to Order.

Father created society. A paradise.

So what was this?

The ground was black; the air was thick.

The only thing Abel recognized was the sky: it shone ruby red, and puffed pink clouds.

The streets were nothing like home. Houses that might have been huge and beautiful were desolate, decayed.

The people were worse.

One hardly looked like a man, but a dark, ragged skeleton. His cough rattled the empty air as he begged the shadows for mercy.

Was this the price of freedom?

Abel had never seen suffering. His heart broke.

Then it opened.

"What can I do for you?" he knelt next to the sick man.

"Liquid!" came the moan.

Abel always had a pouch of hydration on his ankle and raised it for the man to drink. The victim was transformed, his aggravation at ease.

"Thank you, thank you, may the Father bless you." The man's eyes steadied on Abel's face. "Do I know you?"

"Please," now Abel begged. "You must tell me what happened here. What terrible place is this?"

"It's Mars!"

"It can't be! I grew up on Mars. It's nothing like this! I only came here because I was looking for my brother."

"Where did you come from?"

Abel told him of the Mars he knew, the home he grew up in, the Father who loved him.

Then the man told him the truth.

***

"I thought I knew you! Dear boy, I was your tutor, the one you loved so much. I fell ill, so they sent me away. Your Father will not permit disease in his palace. He will not even give people the time to heal.

He's not a bad man. Everything he's done is out of love for you. But love can inspire terrible actions.

Your Father did not create Mars, but he did save it. Long ago, the kings and queens of another world made Mars their home. They were full of greed and guile, and their era was one of decadence. Then two gods of destruction

201

came and wiped out everything. Only your Father's and his Brother's clans survived.

His brother was a wicked man, the first to come to Mars, and the worst of all of them. He ran deep into Space with his followers before the others even knew of their fate. He brings his own curse with him.

Your Father collected as many survivors as he could and protected them until the gods dispersed. Then he set about creating a new society, a safe society, where there would be no greed, no death, no violence.

But paradise comes at a price."

Abel's stomach twisted.

"A lady told me I had a brother."

"You still do."

***

He told him where to go and how to get there.

He didn't tell him what to expect.

The longer Abel walked in this new world, the more he knew he could never go back. The only way was forward.

Abel found the house his tutor described—a grubby shack neighbouring a forlorn forest.

A man with skin the same shade as Abel's exited the hovel to dispose a bucket of refuse. He was bent over like a question mark, his tan face covered with strange grooves. Abel had never seen a face like that before. Everyone back home had skin that was taut and smooth.

The man saw Abel, dropped his bucket, and ran to him.

"Are you…?" Abel began, but his question was answered with a hug.

Somehow he'd always known Father hadn't made him by blood. But this brother was a part of Abel, and Abel, a part of him.

His heart leapt higher than the tree he'd had to climb.

***

Inside, Abel sat on a dirty chair at a dirty table while his kin poured him a dirty cup of water he was too polite to reject.

"I can't believe it." his brother gaped. "I never thought I'd see you again!"

"You remember me?"

"Of course! But you don't, do you. Father must have erased me from your mind. It would have been easier that way. For you and for him."

"How can we be brothers? You don't look like me."

"We age faster out here. Or, more accurately, you age slower in there." Abel's brother sipped his own cup with sardonic satisfaction. "Father took every precaution."

Abel didn't know what "age" meant, but there were more pressing questions.

"Why did he get rid of you?"

A long sigh widened Brother's ribs.

"I think he saw himself in you and his brother in me. Father isn't a bad man. You must understand that. I can't begrudge him. I'm too old to be bitter. It's a waste of time."

His eyes welled.

"I'm glad I got to see you before I died."

***

Abel didn't know what death was either, but he soon found out.

His brother was frail and at peace, which made for a swift departure from the world. When Abel watched the light leave his brother's eyes, it dawned on him the inevitability of all things. How could he say which things were good and which were bad? How could he separate himself from all the agony and ecstasy of the world like his Father had?

He could not retrace his steps.

He had to move forward.

He kissed his brother goodbye and headed for the forest.

"Don't go that way!" warned a woman. "It's wilderness!"

Abel answered, "It's better than this."

He stripped bare. He even left his hydration pouch behind. He was content to become dust.

The forest was quiet and whole. Birds waddled, flies buzzed. Only here did Abel see the beauty of imperfection.

He grew thirsty but didn't drink. His hunger increased. And when fatigue arrived, he rested his head on the largest tree in the centre of the wood, but didn't sleep.

He didn't give up, but he surrendered.

Paradise was on its way, and when it came, it wouldn't have walls.

CAGED BIRDS DON'T SING

You know nothing of Hell—yet.

You may have heard a little about the Big City, and even less of Limbo, but these are the places where real stories simmer, steaming up our mortal windows.

It's possible you've heard of a girl called V, though I wouldn't expect her infamy to reach your circles (again, yet). By now she'd been caged (literally) in the New Bar, forever doomed to hear music she couldn't play.

V was a DJ, among other things, but all you really need to know is she had more than one albatross around her neck, and would do anything to remove them.

There are few heroes among the dead. Limbo has some, but they're too busy for this story, which means we're stuck with the vagrants.

Mick's Death Age was -36.7 (don't even try to do the math). He was one of those rare few in Limbo fixated on his life more than his death.

Every Limbonese has unfinished business, usually owing to their untimely demise. Suicide, bombings, choking in one's vomit—all these exits necessitate a Limbo visit. It's meant to be a temporary stay, but most folks never leave.

Mick wasn't preoccupied with how he died, but who he left behind. He wasn't a user, abuser, emo chick, or rockstar misogynist like most Limbo clientele. Once upon a patriarchy, Mick was a good Catholic boy who wanted a better life for his family, which, to him, meant separation from Britain—but that's a story you can easily find on the internet.

Now you understand his nickname, but you don't understand why you could find him with OJ any day of the week (and Limbo weeks are *long*).

OJ was your more typical Limbo fare: an angry, sad kid who died from booze and/or disappointment. She kicked it wearing her "Ulster is British" t-shirt, if that's any indication. Yet she and Mick were thick as thieves—no, thicker, because they no longer bothered with stealing things but people.

OJ and Mick were notorious kidnappers, which is exactly why V summoned them to her cage on a dreary Tuesday that was like every other Tuesday in Limbo (or any other day, for that matter).

"So this is where they're keeping you," Mick sat at the edge of V's bars.

V looked like a caged bird who wouldn't sing as much as peck your eyes out.

"You've never been in here, then?"

"Who the hell wants to go to a club where you're not allowed to dance?" OJ scoffed, loudly, almost loud enough to hide her delight in the funk bouncing through the speakers.

"Yep." V conceded, "Limbo loves its irony."

Mick watched her with wise, weary eyes.

"I know you, V."

"Join the club."

"I remember when I first saw you. With Shae. You were inseparable. Then that whole thing with the pixies and the zombies…what happened, exactly?"

"I didn't invite you here for some fucking retrospective." Mick was lucky V wasn't allowed to throw glass anymore. "I want to enlist you."

"Enlist us?" OJ hailed a server and mouthed, "Three gin-and-gasolines."

"I want you to kidnap me."

This caught OJ's attention.

"Oh yeah?" she sneered. "For what ransom?"

V's eye roll would knock over a rhinoceros. OJ was unmoved. If anything, it made her giggle harder.

"Sorry, princess. We just don't get many people wanting to kidnap *themselves*."

"And," Mick lowered his voice at the approach of the waiter, "isn't it a little risky to discuss this here?"

"Where else am I going to go?" V challenged, sipping her beverage through a plastic straw in a plastic cup. "I got one of my old bartenders to slip me some Eave's Drop. Anyone listens in, they'll just hear us talking about the weather."

OJ scoffed twice within a sixty-second span. "The weather? But it's the same every day!"

"Which, to be fair, does make it a conversation piece," Mick returned to the question mark hanging in the air. "Fine. You want to be kidnapped. To what end?"

"What do you think? I want out!"

Even though discretion was moot, Mick was compelled to fold his hands on the table and lean in, like one of those old bishops he used to know.

"Kid. The Power Beams rule this town. They've actually made it a nice place to Unlive. They'd catch you in a second, drop you right back here."

"Or somewhere worse," volunteered OJ.

"I'm well aware of what those goody-goodies are capable of," V's bitterness could have stopped an elephant. OJ didn't care.

"So why fight 'em? Mick and I are basically retired. With the Power Beams around, crime costs you. I'm learning pottery, for fuck's sake!"

"I don't just want out of my prison. I want out of Limbo. Entirely."

You know how people complain how sighs in stories are unrealistic? (I just sighed twice writing that, but whatever.) Well, if you're averse to sighs, you'll definitely struggle to believe that both OJ and Mick choked on their G&Gs.

"What, you think we have some goddamn Hades' chariot? Which would only take you to Hell, by the way."

"OJ's right, V. Where else is there?"

It was V's turn to lean in.

"A Better Place."

Lucky that Mick and OJ had already put down their drinks.

"For fuck's sake, that's where we all wanna get! But good fucking luck doing it."

"Right again, OJ. Sorry, V. Apart from waiting around for your Spiritual Social Work, the only way to a Better Place is, well…"

"Working on yourself," OJ chewed a pencil stub (in case you haven't heard, Limbo doesn't have cigarettes). "And who the hell wants to do that?"

"You two did! I know the story. Mick was in the IRA—"

"That's never been proven!"

"And you! You're certainly not called "OJ" because you dig Vitamin C!"

"Vitamin what?"

"And you're best friends! That's got to indicate some kind of growth, don't you think? I know firsthand that friendship makes the burden of Limbo a little lighter. That means your vibration is already aligned to Somewhere Better. With your energy, and my desire, we'll find a way."

"V," Mick looked more like a father than a criminal, "there's no back door to Heaven."

On V's face, there was almost something like a smile.

"We'll see."

***

The kidnapping was planned for 7:15 PM on the second Tuesday of the week, but since there's no watches in Limbo (or calendars), OJ and Mick had to improvise.

"I've been thinking of what V said," OJ confided (OJ didn't confide to anyone but Mick).

"Yeah?"

"Can friendship really get us to a Better Place?"

"Honestly, kid? I think it already has."

I won't bore you with the kidnapping. Let's just say when bars are too hard to break, you have no choice but to get soft.

I'll admit OJ and Mick looked pretty silly trying to mop up a puddle while security demanded to know where V was, though for all intents and purposes, V was Nowhere.

"I can't believe you had *Cyane's tears* in your old bar!!!" even OJ was excited. She whispered to a bottle under her coat while Mick advised the map.

A little voice replied,

"*I* can't believe the Power Beams were too stupid to check my stash after the fire. Plenty magical items are flame-retardant. Even when it's blue flame."

"What happened with all that, anyway?"

"Yet another walk down memory lane, and I don't have legs."

"Okay, ladies!" Mick rolled up the papyrus. "First things first, we'll need a portal."

"Nooo," OJ set down the vial of V, "I suck at portals!"

"I don't," V offered. "Just give me a minute to materialize."

"We can't make it here, anyway. We'll have to go to the art gallery."

"The what?"

The art gallery is one of the least popular spots in Limbo, second only to the Hills of Meditation. Most people spend their death at bars or parties and can't leave even when they want to.

Like the Meditation Hills, the art gallery sits on a slightly higher plain than the rest of Limbo (art always helps us reach a Better Place). This was the logic that brought our trio thither, V wringing out her tresses until they were solid again.

"Nice trick, princess!" OJ remained impressed.

"Yeah, well. It's no good unless there's someone around to mop you up. And it's weakening. I'll be vulnerable for a while. You'll have to watch me."

"No worries, princess. I got your back."

"Would you stop calling me that?"

"Nope!"

"C'mon, ladies! Time to find us a painting."

OJ groaned, "This is no time for a tour, Mick!"

"I wasn't planning on it. A painting is one of the best entry spots for portals. The stronger the energy of the painting, the stronger the portal will be. But the stronger the painting, the harder it is to make a portal in the first place."

"This is no time for riddles, either!"

"It's not a riddle, OJ! It's just how these things work."

V wasn't having it.

"We don't have time to do it right. We just need to do it."

"I don't think that's a good idea, V."

"Fuck off, old man! You want everything perfect and right and nice? I spent my whole life being nice, and look where it got me!"

"Yeah well," OJ came to her pal's defence, "from what I've heard, you sure as hell stopped being nice once you were dead."

"Shut up and help me find a shitty painting!"

This is not as easy as it sounds. The whole point of bad art is to trick the viewer into thinking there's value when there's just a corporate bottom line or shiny algorithm. Bad art is sometimes prettier than the real thing, but it's the prettiness that deprives it of soul.

It's easy to forget how pretty V was, her face so often distorted with derision or despair. Yet, at this moment, as she tore through the gallery with blind ferocity, her beauty shone through.

"Ooh, here! This is shit for sure."

"That's a Matisse, OJ."

"Yeah. Real shit!"

"Maybe you should sit this part out."

"Call off the search!" V sounded satisfied. "I've got your bad art right here."

OJ and Mick gathered round.

"You sure?" Mick wondered.

"Definitely." V conferred.

"But he was very popular. Still is."

"Yeah, but he was a total misogynist."

"Like all painters…"

"No, no, I'm sure of this one. Just feel it. The vibe's so… low."

Mick had to agree.

"But," OJ cautioned, "with a painting this low, how can it get you to Somewhere Better? Isn't that the whole point of aiming high?"

"Don't you worry. My passion will get the portal on track."

V had many flaws, but they were nothing compared to her passions. She could talk about music forever, and if she still had any friends, that's what she'd be doing. She could gush about funk and moon over punk, debate remixes, critique covers, analyze playlists and recite the discography of just about any band from the 1960s to Eternity. Perhaps if she'd been given a better outlet, or even some opportunities, she never would have ended up in Limbo's art gallery conducting a portal to take her as far away as possible.

I won't bore you with the portal-making process. Suffice to say, it's easier to get where you don't want to go than somewhere you do.

In V's case, she didn't get anywhere, but she did get something.

Mick and OJ saw her dissolve. She even glowed! It looked like everything would be okay. Then, she was flung back like something chewed on her but didn't like the taste. Her eyes rolled, her head spun, and Mick smelled something on her that reminded him of the Troubles: like burnt rubber, and worse.

"Uh, V? Where were you?"

"I gotta try again!" already V was peeling herself off the floor. She'd had worse headaches than this.

"Where were you, V?"

"Nowhere! Just a weird, swirling mess."

"You were In-Between."

"I guess."

"You can pick up things when you're In-Between."

"Is there a point to this?"

Mick grabbed her by the hair.

"What the fuck, you lousy prick!!" by the time V shoved him off, he had already collected the evidence on his hand: a dark patch of ash from the base of her neck.

"What's that?"

"A mark. You've got a Watcher."

"SHIT!"

Imagine a gorilla the size of a large cat, only instead of the usual humble visage of that simian, black, razor teeth so sharp they look animatronic, and glowing red eyes that fill you with all-seeing dread. It may almost remind you of a grinning organ grinder monkey, had he been baptized in Hellwater.

The curse of the Watcher is simple. Wherever you go, it follows. Wherever you look, it will be. There is no escape from its gaze, unless you're able to give it a kiss—a feat no one has yet achieved.

Unlike you, OJ was unacquainted with the above paragraphs, and failed to understand the Watcher's significance.

"Who cares? Something's "watching" us, we'll bash it."

"You can't. Only she can see it."

Of course, she already could. It rested on a picture's frame, ever watchful. She moved her gaze to the floor, and there it stood.

Soon, it would be all she could see.

You may be surprised that the Watcher has driven all its prey mad before anyone could kiss it. But who among us can love what they loathe?

I won't waste too much time on V's meltdown. I'm sure your imagination can take care of it.

"I'm sorry, V." OJ even tried to rest a hand on V's shoulder; V opted to hide under OJ's arm instead. "I said I'd watch you. I'm really sorry."

"It was just bad luck!" Mick insisted.

"It's not your fault. And it's not luck. It's what I get for trying to run out on myself. Just like I run out on everything."

She dipped to the floor, where the Watcher was waiting. She covered her face, but could see its stare through her fingers.

"If only I hadn't come here."

"Well," Mick reasoned, "we could take you back."

"What?"

"Look. The PBs would have probably caught up with us anyway. And there's zero chance someone like you could sneak into Heaven, even without that monkey on your back. No offence."

"None of this is helping."

"Listen a minute! We could turn you in. Insist that, in order to stop future escape attempts, they need to do what they should have done in the first place and magic-proof your cage!"

"Then…"

"As long as you're behind those bars, the Watcher won't reach you."

OJ rolled her lips for a long time.

"Those aren't great options, Mick."

"Sometimes all you get are shitty options. It's our task to pick the least shitty one."

V tried opening her eyes, but the Watcher's vile gaze made her close them again.

***

They returned V to her prison at 12:06 AM, but since nobody had a watch, all they knew was that it was late. OJ blindfolded V as a courtesy, even though soon the Watcher would be visible even when her eyes were closed.

Sometimes the hard road is the only one you can follow. If we don't make the right choice for ourselves, the universe tends to make it for us.

Safely de-magicked, V was free from the Watcher's menacing stare. It waited beyond those bars, but that was a problem she could face another day. For now, she could only hope to work on herself, for that's the only way you can get to a Better Place.

It wasn't all bad, really.

At least she'd made some friends.

CAT IN A TREE

I'm going to Hell.

It'll be a short trip.

Shelly and Byron have ignored me for weeks. The last thing Byron said was, "Go to Hell!"

So I will.

Maps can get you any place. You only need the right one.

Most app stores are online; I had to visit this one in person. It looked (and smelled) like my grandma's closet: all browns and pinks, creepy ornaments and candy wrappers.

A creature twelve inches tall with skin like a coconut shell was enthroned behind the partition, bolstered by a precarious tower of books and bric-a-brac.

His voice was like a squeaky toy talking into a tin can.

"Here for an app?"

"I guess."

His eyes resembled black olives. They halved while he peered at me.

"You a witch?"

"What? Me? No."

"Good. I don't like 'em. But you're human?"

"Yes."

"How'd you find this place?"

"A guy."

"A witch?"

"No."

"Good," he shuffled from one side of his teetering pillar to another. "What do you need?"

"A map to Hell."

"Well, that's easy. It's accessorizing for the trip that's difficult," his fingers tickled book spines. "You'll need protection. A Cronus sickle, invisibility cap, maybe some Medean balm…"

"I don't need protection."

"Isn't this a rescue mission?"

"Nope." I stared straight into his freaky face. "This is a move."

Thank god he didn't ask why. Who can explain how quickly love can be traded for hate?

They hate me. They should.

What kind of parent would do what I did?

The app took a while to install. It even left soot on the charging port.

I hate phones; I only had this one because I bought it for Dad, who rejected it—like everyone rejects my attempts to make things better.

***

Hell can be found by way of the ravine.

217

Weird. You'd think the door to Hades would be in the financial district, guarded by the mob boss of a child porn ring. Through a dumpster. Or a toilet. Next to the bench where Morrison proposed to me.

Directions to Hell:

A) 9804 Dun Street

to

B) Hell (Portal Zone B)

+ Add Destination

via the low road/Needle Park Greenway (23 min.)

-Head South on Dun Street

-Turn Left onto E 9th Street

-Turn Right onto the Road Paved With Good Intentions

-Follow the Long and Winding Road Where the Streets Have No Name

-Pass the Boulevard of Broken Dreams Just Around the Riverbend

Destination will be on the right.

The ravine is resplendent in winter. I love how my boots crunch.

Byron and Shelly used to take their slides down near the river, where that perfect arc opens up on the ice. I used to beg them not to, back when I still got things right.

Being a mother is impossible. No matter what you do, you're damned.

I'm Just Around the Riverbend when I hear:

"Help! Help!"

I must be getting close.

A lady runs at me, arms spread like she's attempting a vertical snow angel.

"Ohthankgod!"

"What's wrong?"

"It's my dog! He's fallen into the river and the ice is too slippery for him to climb back up and—"

The canine's cries compete with her own: yelps of pain punctuated with terror.

"Please! You have to help!"

My app beeps at me:

Warning: Hell portal closes in 15 minutes.

She stares at my phone like it's the Titanic's last lifeboat.

"Could you phone emergency?"

"I'm sorry," I slip the cell away, "Really sorry, but I'm in a hurry."

"Please! I don't have a phone! You have to help! My dog—"

"It's just an animal!" I push her back as she tries to grab me. "Just an animal!" I say again, more to myself than her. "It's not the end of the world."

The dog's shrieks echo against the unforgiving ice. The woman's tears chap her face.

"Please."

***

She waited with her pet; I waited for the firefighters at the parking lot.

It looked like they brought the whole calvary.

They looked suited up for war.

I watched their important backs recede while I pointed the way, as ineffectual as Plato pointing to heaven.

Beep:

Warning: Hell portal closes in 2 minutes.

I always get death anxiety. You start to think making the first move will render the dread impotent.

"Thanks for helping out," the chief interrupts my soliloquy.

He misinterprets my tears as concern for someone other than myself.

"Don't worry! The dog will be fine. He'll probably have frostbite, but—"

"It's not that," I sit; so does he. "It's just…animals! They're such a pain."

"They can be."

"I gave their cat away."

"Sorry?"

"Their cat. The stupid cat my ex-husband bought my kids. It wasn't…I didn't do it to get back at him. Really. I know that's what the kids think but the reality is that cat was pissing *everywhere*! I'd come home to find the counter covered in piss, the plants dead from piss, Byron's hockey bag soaked in piss…I'd be trying to get the kids ready for school and it would be pissing in their shoes!

Maybe I should have taken it to the vet. But I don't have that kind of money."

I'd wipe my nose, but the cold will take care of it.

"So I took the cat away. To a farm outside the City. The lady said it could be a mouser.

But I didn't tell the kids until after. They just came downstairs one morning and the cat was gone."

"Ah."

"They hate me. I know I fucked up. But it was only an animal. It was only—"

Beep:

Warning: Hell portal closes in 1 minute.

Sartre was wrong.

Hell isn't other people.

Hell is me.

"I should go."

"Wait," he reaches for my hand,

"Don't you want to see the dog?"

GUESS WE'RE WALKING

The boy was cold.

The girl was bent over 'cause of that new strain of BFT that for some reason turned people into hunchbacks.

Or she was cold too.

The boy was white. The girl, Native. The boy's sign read,

"Need Help God Bless."

The girl had no sign.

Tenderly, painfully, he kissed her lips and tucked a tuft of trembling hair behind her ear.

He sang in her ear, too.

"Let us on bus driver

Let us on bus driver!

Let us on bus driver

All we wanna do is get to the West End…"

She laughed, painfully, tenderly. It was their favourite Armstrong song, adapted for their present circumstance.

Money spent. Drugs out.

Cold.

They had to get to the West End. His brother would put them up, at least for the night, and even if he had no B, he'd have something to fend off their demons (for a while).

The boy smelled. The girl couldn't tell. They politely ignored the other boy who had joined them, sketched out on some other drug scene. His sign was half of a cardboard box.

It read,

"to ugly to prostitute

to dume to steal

asking helps please :)"

He had a phone, probably stolen, and hunched over it, looking up who knows what, probably nothing, his lopsided teeth easily mistaken for a grin, but he was cold too.

The bus came. The Normies, who had kept a wide berth, lined up obediently.

"C'mere, lil' darling," the boy pulled her in and sang another Armstrong fav, this time from his Rancid days,

"She's automatic

So automatic

The way that she moves

The way that she mo-o-oves…"

They met at a Rancid concert: some anniversary tour, back before he lost his construction job, before concerts got too expensive. He remembered how she looked: all bright, eyes open.

He would always remember her like that.

She remembered little from that night except how the crowd broke over her like a tide, how she was sure she broke a rib in the mosh pit, how a sweet white boy helped her up so she wouldn't get crushed.

He could have been a singer.

She could have been anything.

The line was disappearing. The wind was picking up.

They knew what to do. Pretend to look for, and fail to find, their transfers. Make a little eye contact (not too much) with the bus driver. The boy would talk if talking had to be done (always let the white boy talk).

It was all good. The drivers always let them on. Sometimes from compassion (The Big City was cold that year), but usually 'cause they were scared of this boy and this girl, even though the bus driver had a family, a house, a home, somewhere to go and nothing to fear, whereas she and he had everything to fear and no protection but each other.

They let everyone else on, including the thug and his elaborative sign.

Their turn.

Hot air hit their faces like paradise, or some other place they'd never go.

Heat was well worth the humiliation of begging the driver for a ride.

The only problem: there was no driver.

The seat was still there, but where a human who may exhibit compassion or fear would usually sit was a robot, designed to be neither attractive nor welcoming. It looked like a Star Wars droid. All joints, no expression.

Even though it had no eyes, they knew they couldn't sneak past it.

It couldn't sympathize with their plight or be duped by their charade. It could only steer, stop, and say with someone else's voice,

"Please insert card or change."

"Oh." said the boy.

"So…" said the girl.

"Please insert card or change."

They went back the way they came:

into the cold.

ONE LAST STOP

I told him not to trust you.

Do you hate me for that?

So what if you do. It was true! I knew the moment I saw you. Slutty dress. Ridiculous shoes. That smile I've seen too many times on too many faces: a deer trying to make friends with headlights.

Is this what it's like for everyone? Are we together in our aloneness? The geese float away with the river, strangely immune to anxiety. WE'RE fucked. We freak out at cobwebs in the face, skeletons in the closet. Monkeys may wage war, but they don't drop bombs! What the fuck's the matter with us? We manufacture shoes that light up when a kid runs, yet we can't figure out how to love thy fucking neighbour. We divert rivers/soul paths. We miss the ones who hurt us.

We ache for them.

FUCK NO, I'm not saying I miss you! I'm just saying…

I know what it's like to hurt so hard it's all you feel.

Even when attacked from all sides, you got allies: least of all the warrior in your heart.

I KNOW it sounds like bullshit! Just give me a chance. I'm trying to…shit. Got a cigarette? Cheers.

What I'm trying to say is I'm exhausted. I've seen too many dreams not only broken but cracked open and left to die on the pavement. Too many bruises, split lips, wilted breasts, too many girls who never made it to women, too many women who could have made a difference. I've seen enough ignorance to know the importance of education. I've known enough cruelty to understand kindness is essential.

That's what I'm trying for, kid. Kindness. It might not look it, but we all dress up our hearts differently.

I used to believe pain held us together. Really, it's the moments. Falling calendars. Mosh pits. When we fall down. When we hold each other up.

I tried to help you. Everyone did.

NO, I'm not telling you to stay! Just think for a minute. Say you get through. What then? This ain't a rom-com! And even if it were, only the men are allowed to be crazy.

Quit revving the motor. Cars have feelings too.

YES, I've been meditating. When life's shit there's nothing to do but try to work at it.

You get that, don't you?

I never liked you. The feeling's probably mutual. Doesn't matter. We're connected. Him, me, you. Everyone, everywhere. And damn do we need each other.

You need me.

I need you.

FUCK, not again! I KNOW you think I kicked you out, but you did that to yourself!

Listen! You think you're some glossy angel in disguise, but you got too much bile for that gig.

You're a shadow-worker, kid. You got the deadly touch, evil eye, whatever you wanna call it. Is that better than being a victim?

It ain't.

Unless you stay and fight.

He ran, okay? From you, this, me, everyone, all of it, and I guess we can't blame him, but if everyone runs, what'll happen to this place?

Folks like us—the girls, the geeks, the freaks, queerdos, subs, dykes, the pleasers, the pussies, the nerds, losers and lepers and whores and dreamers with a list of rejections longer than their spine and dark circles darker than the new moon's light—we got a different destiny. We lack the luxury of giving up, running off to somewhere better.

We choose this because we must.

It's our duty to stay.

It's our duty to survive.

YOU'VE GOTTA HANG ON TO ME; I'M TIRED OF LOSING*

this is an ode to the wild ones with the wild looks and wild eyes
the ones who'd fare better in wilderness if they weren't so damn tired.
they called brando the wild one but that kid was a zoo-kept leopard
im talking about the lepers who bark at snow and slide on ice who
can't but maybe could've if someone had given them the chance.
here's a toast to the lost boys the wives in the bible without names
spare a thought for the glue horse the dropped course the rigged games
(and all those suckers who play anyway.)
when i say wild i mean punch lines off time
kids who can't dance audience that won't clap
the age lines, the last in line.
when i say wild i mean writers 'cause real writers can't be tamed
we sweat and we scream and pretend to collab but really compete
'cause there's only one man left standing and he's seldom the one
we wanted to win but he matched the hashtags of his time and
stayed just enough in line for folks to colour him in.
i guess i'm saying we've all got a little wild in us you need it for such a
wild ride like this the kind that pulls you off and apart as you try to weave words

together
transmute agony into bliss———
so save a place for the sad fucks with bad luck and bad tattoos who
were on the run but their knees gave out 'cause bad boys grow old too.
raise your glass to the bad girls who get ugly fast from too much fun
and the good girls
who keep it together
as it all falls apart around them.

title taken from They Shoot Horses, Don't They?

BORN MEAT

—a novelette

"Our lives are in themselves the story of animals."

—Ocean Vuong

1 : HUNGER

A slaughterhouse is easy for the workers. Herding, breeding, killing: simple parts to a simple process to export goods, import wealth, and supply the demand for flesh.

Spread the feed. Tag the ears. Play your part, do your work, leave with a paycheque.

For us, it was different.

For us, being herded, bred, and killed was less of a routine and more of a nightmare. We are sensitive animals and can account for nothing more beyond that realm. We have no facts, only feelings.

I heard the workers talk—"prime A", "livestock"—but so little made sense. I was in no place to reason or rationalize. We were not granted the luxury of denial. We had no say in our own value.

We didn't wield the knives, lock the cages, shovel the waste, scrape blood from the ceiling. We weren't the producers.

We were the product.

My first memory is my mother. She only had room to lay on her side, legs curled and bent. She was overweight; her nipples were raw and wilted. Sometimes she'd kick at the bars or groan at the walls, but she was usually somewhere else—somewhere better.

I don't remember my birth—I'm sure few do. I retain disjointed sensations: searing cold, howling air, and a trembling body—my own.

I had no idea of the hell I was being born into. To be fattened and feasted upon—what child could predict such a destiny? I was but a baby: tiny, pink, struggling to blink. I only longed for my mother's embrace. Her moist, warm milk.

The floor was cold. I had three brothers and three sisters. They were born sluggish and slow as we were bred to be, but I was cursed with awareness.

Beastly lights battered down on me. Rancid stench flared my nostrils. All the mothers were mad. They babbled; they chewed off their tongues. There was a monster lurking in these pens, one with a thirst for blood.

No one understood how this world had come to be. No one could remember a time outside these walls. We were only animals. How could we understand our punishment? Would it have lessened the pain to know we were innocent?

At first my siblings couldn't speak. They'd grunt, huff, snort, sniff, and oh, did they cry! I took quickly to speech (they'd bred us to age fast, too), and my mother was grateful for my mind: it meant she had someone to talk to.

When lucid, my mother was brilliant and beautiful. She was my source of life, my love, my warmth and growth. How could I begrudge her? She only did what she could.

She told me tales of kindness. She told me stories of our ancestors who lived long and wild and free. Freedom—what a word!

It ruined me. It gave me hope.

These were only myths, and myths do little to qualm reality. Her stories barely braced us for our antibiotic haze. We were suffocated in this claustrophobic space, but her words gave us some room.

Through all this carnage, these sordid sights, not one of my brethren attempted escape.

Dreams are a privilege rarely granted to slaves. They were only taught to submit.

When I first saw those muck-covered stalls and unfeeling iron bars, one miniature morsel among many, I knew that I must change my destiny.

Strange, how living souls are pushed upon our paths. My mission started small: a thimble of water in an ocean.

Rebellion is a dangerous fantasy and dangers take time to grow. In those first days all I wanted was my mother's milk, and more importantly, her affection.

It started with a hug. Or rather, a lack of one.

A mother's voice is more than enough. But I wanted more: I wanted to feel the beat of her heart against my own. This was the embrace I craved, a raw longing so deeply ingrained. I was desperate for connection.

This is the worst part of instinct: to have needs recognized though unmet.

I'm sure mother wanted to hold me. Those empty, aching eyes told me so. She wanted nothing more than to lean her swollen face on my rosy, wrinkled cheek.

But we couldn't reach. Metal bars impeded her from reaching us. Only her breasts were available: a dispensary on which we could feed.

This was "for our own safety" (some mothers had attempted to eat their own young). Yet I knew my mother would never hurt me.

When she didn't tell me stories, she would apologize.

"I'm sorry I can't hold you. I'm sorry I can't protect you. I'm sorry, I'm sorry…"

And she'd cry so long and loud that her voice would blend into the din.

Mothers have instincts of their own. It was her duty to protect us from the world's hunger, but her cage debilitated her. She could only watch and wonder what went wrong.

I didn't want her apologies. I wanted her close.

I nudged her again; I tried to reach her neck. My brothers and sisters fought over breakfast; I was the only one asking my mother for answers. Was I more of a burden than a blessing?

"Mother, mother, when can we leave? This doesn't feel right. It doesn't feel like home."

She closed her eyes as if darkness would erase reality.

"Home doesn't exist."

More questions cluttered my mind, but my mother was too weary to continue our talk.

"Sit still, little one," she sighed, "Just close your eyes, hold your breath, and drink."

The word was an ugly place. It might have been easier had I been quick to succumb, but I didn't. I couldn't. Even as she told me to rest, my heart screamed. Somehow I found the courage to dream.

I didn't want to get used to this. This cramped space, foul stench, all things cold and hard and wrong. I could not abide this madness. My life had value, if only to me.

It was only after all my family had gotten their fill that I decided to suckle. Mother's milk warmed my insides, and for a moment life was luxury. All the unearthly metal melted away; joy sprouted from the ground.

In my mind, I saw things I shouldn't have known: colours that comforted, shapes that deceived. I'd see perfect green, infinite blue, and think, "Is this insanity?"

We grew up fast. My limbs longed to stretch, bend, and run, but there was no room. My muscles were weak, my joints inflamed, my extremities caked with sores.

One night, my mother was more nervous than usual. Her depression gave way to relentless agitation.

I asked yet another question likely to reveal a terrible truth.

"Mother, what's wrong?"

Eyes darted, trembles emanated.

"They're coming soon. I know it!"

"Who are they?"

"They. The big ones. The shadows."

I wanted to run from the shadow and crash into the light, out of the cold and into the heat, out of the terror and into peace.

"What do they want?"

"They want to kill us."

Frantic shrieks sounded off the walls. It was only after they silenced I realized they came from me. Even the young know of death, though we want nothing to do with it.

I didn't want to die. I wanted to be.

"They're going to come," she cried, "and they're going to take you away. I've had many children, many times. They always take them away. I shudder to think of their fate. Was I just born to breed? Were you just born to die?"

I hung my head with someone else's shame.

Who would steal a child from their mother?

Was this nature? Was this normal?

Was this right?

One thing was sure: I had to arm myself against the monsters.

2 : HORROR

The sounds were far away at first.

Then they enveloped me.

Hands, hands, overwhelming hands! I couldn't fight; I was limp and meek. All I could think was, "I don't want to leave my mother."

I wish I'd had the chance to say goodbye.

I wish I could have saved her.

I begged my brothers and sisters to fight with me. One whispered back, "What's the point? This is how it is. How it's always been. May as well accept it."

Another floor, another crate. At least we had room to crawl. The lights were bright, the floor was cold. Was the whole world made of cages?

My siblings were distraught. They were dizzy, sick, and lost. Some succumbed to faints while others clawed and gnawed at the bars—not to attempt escape, but as a fleeting outlet to their agitation. Others turned their teeth on themselves.

Torn from our mother, we were adrift.

They came for us again.

This time, we were separated.

Our hands were held down.

Our mouths were held open.

Click. Click. Click.

One of the monsters approached with a metal instrument in their hands. It winked horridly against the light.

I didn't know what it was, but it looked like it would hurt.

The tool clamped over my teeth.

Was that me screaming?

Was it someone else?

Or was it all of us?

I longed to hide under my mother's legs. I wanted to feel love again.

Then they reached under my flank. There was a rip, a shower of blood, and my scream was the only thing left in the world. I'd never known pain could be so real. I never knew pain could take over reality.

I longed for something to numb the ache, ease the peril.

We were returned to our cages. What incredible loneliness in a sea of bodies! Two of my brothers died from the shock of their mutilations. Flies ate at their eyes for days: more souls ripped from the universe.

The world went quiet, and stayed that way. I forced myself to move however I could. I found strength where I thought I had none. I only ate what I needed, and when they shoved more muck down my throat, I spat it back up in defiance. My fellow inmates fattened, but I stayed slim.

The frigid floor became my friend. Though my body adapted to these harsh conditions, my heart refused to harden. My head swelled with empathy. My soul burned. Detachment had kept me alive, but feeling was all that would help me survive.

Is it a blessing or a curse to feel so much in such an unfeeling world? Is it easier to feel nothing at all?

We rarely saw the walking shadows, except when they came to clean our cages or spread our feed. Younglings were added to our repertoire, yet as our population escalated, the size of our pen refused to increase. Even in such confined quarters, the clipping of our teeth and removal of our nails guaranteed we couldn't hurt each other. Sometimes I'd still have memories of that wrenching twinge in my mouth, and shudder.

More often, I'd think of my mother. What she said, what she felt, how she hurt. I'd consider her words, her complete disregard of hope, and her most ominous premonition. Was she right? Fear scratched my bones, stole my sleep, and weakened my appetite.

Our overlords were unkind, uncaring beasts. They only knew violent touches: smacks, shouts, kicks.

They wouldn't even listen when I tried to speak to them.

It was odd. I understood fragments of their language, but they thought us too undeveloped to master speech. I would ever venture to communicate, "Sir? Sir? Please, Sir, my friend is sick. Can you give them something, please?"

Nothing. I may as well have only grunted. I spoke, but they couldn't listen.

I woke scared and slept the same, but was determined to find a light at the end of this dark, twisting tunnel.

If no path existed, I'd have to make my own.

Whenever awake, I would repeat, "I am going to escape this place."

3: HOPE

The time of slaughter was coming. No longer was it a nightmare or a whisper. It grew skin and bones. It gained weight.

Larger inmates in adjacent cells would pace, only to be removed and never return.

My mother was right: they wanted to kill us. They were going to take us away.

They walked by us every day but never saw us—and certainly never saw our misery. They acted like our condition was normal.

Was it?

The others laughed at me when I retold mother's stories, or worse, when I dared divulge my dreams. They'd admonish, "There's no escape! This is all that exists! Grates and crates and blood on the walls."

Our masters thought us unconscious, and in a way, they were right. Too many were resigned to their fate, and pondered nothing but surviving the next moment, lest despair overtake. One can never improve one's situation if one is resigned to the present. Consciousness indicates the ability to expand our awareness beyond what is, and towards what could be.

I was so occupied with my contemplations, I failed to notice a youngling who approached me. His teeth had just been filed, his testicles recently removed. I remembered that terrible ache, and pitied him.

"Where is she? Where is she?" he moaned, and I knew he longed for his mother as I still longed for mine.

His head shook, his body quaked. His eyes were wet with sullied innocence. He collapsed at my side, too agonized to even crawl.

"The air hurts." he wheezed.

I could only hold him in sympathy.

"Our waste hasn't been cleared. The workers take their time cleaning it."

I held him in our purgatory, though it felt much more like Hell.

Could I take this sweet, gentle soul with me when I made my escape? Surely not—he was too frail, lungs clearly infected from the airborne bile. He wouldn't fight off the sickness—or the despair.

"Was it always like this?" he asked.

I chose my words carefully.

"I've seen nothing else. But I have to believe there's more."

"How can you believe?"

"I don't know. It's just a feeling. But a strong one."

Alas, my hope was stronger than him.

Many would succumb, their bodies neglected for days. The scent of death was unrelenting and ubiquitous. I would sometimes lie next to someone who could have been a friend, brooding. Why was I spared, and they condemned. Why did they die while I dreamed.

I even dreamt of grass. I didn't understand what it was at the time, having been born in captivity, but my spirit dared to traverse meadows my body couldn't reach. In my mind, grass was a soft floor of a calming hue and delicious smell. At night, I would travel away to a place where all my family frolicked with me, a place where we were healthy and happy and—oh!—free!

Dreams must end. I would always wake in reality.

You might think it foolish to keep dreaming, keep hoping, but it was my source of survival. It gave me a reason to fight.

I differed from my compatriots in my intelligence and tenacity, but our desires were ultimately the same. We wanted warmth, companionship. Any one of us would have been happy running through the grass, drinking from a stream, soaking in the sun. Simple needs, yet all denied.

Some artists see their painting before their first stroke. I saw my paradise before I was anywhere near it.

It was difficult. Sometimes, it felt impossible. I longed to fade with the rest. My body and brain screamed for me to give up and give in. Hope was an expensive and exhausting commodity. Yet without it, what would I be? The miseries of our home struck me harder than any of my siblings, yet while many withered, I remained.

There was more to survival than weakness or strength. Perseverance was marked by more than the material. My imagination saved me. Without my fantasies, I may have never dared as I did, and there would have been no tale to tell.

I often escaped with my mind—but what of my body? That was more difficult. The bars were not about to bend, no matter my exertion, nor was a space wide enough for me to squeeze through. How could I know how to get out of here? I was just an animal with a dark brain and good heart.

One thing I had to my advantage: I was slimmer than the others, quicker, and nimbler, for I paced while everyone else only sat and moaned. Yet my lungs too heaved, and my knees were as raw as anyone's. Others would kick, eyes swirling in their heads, indicative of the madness I so feared. Day after day, I resisted its weighty pull. My mind was all I had left, and I wasn't going to let them take that from me.

My brain was my greatest advantage. Our owners thought us harmless, but I knew better.

My mind was active; my body could not yet match its vigour. These were the only tools I had to work with.

I would have to wait until the monsters opened our cage.

They would only open the cage when they came to take us away.

It would be the fight of my life.

Literally.

4 : HOMEWARD

It was time.

Like every morning, I repeated my mantra.

"I am going to escape this place. I am going to escape this place!"

Words felt weak, fake. The walls around me were real, and full of blood.

I persisted, I insisted:

"I am going to escape!"

There were so many more questions, ones my mother hadn't had the time or energy to answer. I was alone to figure things out for myself.

The time for planning, questioning, doubt, and hesitance had passed. Now was the time for action. Now was the time for risk.

I had to trust my heart, and my instincts. These alone could lead me to a better life.

If I fell, at least I would fall fighting. I would not die a victim, and thus, I would die free.

Didn't we all deserve that chance?

If only my remaining brothers, sisters and cousins would rise with me! Imagine the revolution! I became dizzy with the vision of myself and hundreds of others resisting our captors, to march outside these dank walls and claim our future. Like a plant will die without water, a revolution will die without hope. Rebellion needs vision. Vision needs rebellion.

Even had I the guile to convince others to join me, I could not use other souls as fodder for my foolhardiness. I was not a leader; I was a dreamer. A dreamer can only dream for themselves.

There I was, alone though surrounded. The hotly breathing bodies of my brethren made me sweat. Then came the sound I knew well: the monsters were coming to get us.

How is it that terror can never grow stale, no matter its repetition? I should have been numb by now, but cowered with the rest of them.

Fear is, in its own twisted way, trying to protect us. Yet it shatters our focus, weakens our resolve, leeches our spirit. If only we could be brave!

Bravery comes from a reason to fight. The monsters tried to convince us our lives were worthless. My family wouldn't fight; they could barely stand. Only in death did we profit our masters. Only in death were we worth anything to them.

I refused to submit. I would have given up on escape if I thought my life were worthless. My life was all I had to offer. If I died, where would the memory of my mother go? Where would my dreams find housing? Dying after demanding to live was one thing, but dying willingly at an adversary's hands was unacceptable—not to many, but to me.

I knew little of the world. My life—and death—would scarcely make a mark. But it mattered to me—to see, to hear, to feel, to love.

I wanted to fight for the right to dream.

The stomp-stomp-stomp I knew too well rang like an alarm in my heart. In a way, I welcomed the adrenaline. I was tired and sick, but bored. I had a curious brain deadened by this dreary atmosphere. I craved stimulation.

And I would soon get it.

To prepare, I tried to remember my dreams.

My mother was there.

The shadows fell on me.

It was warm.

The cage door creaked. I hung on to my dream.

The ground was full of that thick, soft stuff. And water fell from the air. It made puddles. I splashed in them! Life was good. Things were the way they were meant to be.

My companions awoke as our captors leapt upon us. Their bangs and shouts ripped everyone from whatever weak solace they'd found in sleep. Even I was shocked, though I'd heard them coming. I'd had so much time to prepare, and now, I was powerless.

I reminded myself to concentrate.

My mind would inspire. My heart would guide. My hope would give me strength.

Amidst the chaos, I tried to breathe.

"Concentrate," I whispered "Let the moment come to you. Don't force it. Don't fret. The opportunity will reveal itself. Whatever you do, don't force it."

Panic told me to run as the gate swung. Panic told me to scramble from the workers' hands.

My instincts knew better. My inner wisdom whispered, *not yet.*

Among my kin, I was another hunk of meat, paid no notice or care. The others were shoved, some dragged, some kicked into movement. Some screamed. Some cried. Most were too tired to complain. There was no use reasoning with a beast so brutal as these.

Rough claws landed on my hide. They wanted me to move, but in that moment, I could only shriek. For all my ails, my heart was softer than ever.

My thoughts returned to when I was young and almost innocent. How far away that moment seemed. I remembered the hands that had torn me from my mother, and subjected me to terrible things. Past traumas intensify present ones. Time blurred. Submission clashed with resistance. I didn't know whether to go up, or down. But I knew I couldn't go back.

I had to move forward. I had to turn to the terror. I had to face the fray.

I would give them no satisfaction in seeing my fear. The monsters didn't eat feed or grains. They only fed off us: our blood, our flesh, our fear.

We were herded down the aisle. My heart sunk, for we crawled and crawled, and only saw crates. Maybe the whole world was a cage. Maybe there was no end to our captivity.

My brother next to me crumpled on the floor, racked with weariness. In response, a worker raised a wicked-looking stick from their waist and prodded my friend's ribs. Every stab made a terrible pop and sizzle, followed by a flash that stung my sight. With every jolt, my poor sibling screeched, too feeble to fight back, escape, or move forward. I wanted to maintain composure, but had to protest, "Sir, sir! Leave him alone, please! You're hurting him! Can't you see his pain? Can't you hear his cries? Please stop, please!"

My pleas again went ignored. Why did I even bother to speak? Why should I try? Why not give up here?

Another worker shoved me as a means to compel me forward, and I was forced along with those remaining. I could only look back in terror at my fallen friend, now trampled and prostrate. Even after he faded into the distance, his screams echoed through me.

Again I longed to take a flying leap. My reason calmed me.

This isn't the time. I told myself. *You can't find the moment. The moment will come to you.*

Others fell on our long walk to death. Some dropped down, or panicked, and suffered the consequences. One was hooked through their back. I watched the weapon fall; I saw the flesh pierced. And I saw the eyes of the victim's attacker. Intelligence was surely there, but I saw no hint of empathy.

A trail of blood lead us out of confinement. The life-liquid coated my limbs, and I left behind bloody prints. There was no playing pretend, no daydreaming the walls away. Here with the dead and dying, there was neither bliss nor ignorance.

My lungs pounded; my brain buckled.

Up ahead, the strangest light split through the room. My eyes were bewildered for, like all the others, I'd never before seen the sun. I was dizzy with possibility. My first burst of rays was a dose of hope. It was just what I needed: proof that there was a better place outside these walls.

This was a light not made by monsters. There was a ground not paved.

We were yelled at, whipped at, struck, directed. They wanted the job over and done with. We scuffled ahead at an alarmed pace.

For the first time in my life, I was outside.

Glory! Beauty! Incredible and vast. On the brink of death, I was the happiest I'd ever been.

I was also horrified. Now that I'd been graced with a glimpse of the world, I wasn't going to let it go. I'd fought to keep my panic contained, and it now threatened to breach what common sense I had left. Everyone was jostling, bleating, pulling, pushing. Even the calmest bellows and softest blows stirred us into chaos.

"Not quite yet," I breathed. "Not quite yet."

Cries now came not only from behind, but up ahead. While those from behind pushed ahead to assuage the workers' rage, those at the front fell back desperately. Slaps and shoves abounded; so too shouts and cries. That abusive, grinding din would stay with me forever.

I finally understood why those ahead of me had been screaming so. The monsters were snatching them up one by one. We were throttled only to be thrown into a big, black thing that rumbled like a hungry, growling beast.

I disappeared in the chaos. Apart from the tags on our ears, we were interchangeable. Could I slip away unnoticed?

Of course not. One shadow saw me, arms outstretched, poised to snatch and grab. At first I was stiffened by terror, swept up into a large, sweltering grasp. Resistance was, for a moment, futile.

I remembered my mother. Her love, her milk.

Sound hushed; sensation diminished.

Suddenly, I was immune to the terror all around me.

Were all those nights plotting and planning pointless? Was hope a lie?

Every moment converged into this point of no return: one single line I was destined to cross.

I was about to be thrown into the belly of the beast. I feigned weakness to fool the enemy. Below, my family bustled, skittered, wailed. The anguish was overflowing, the anarchy relentless.

The only body I could control was my own.

Finally, my heart cried, "Now!"

All my terror, my anger, my grief, combined into one determined leap.

I flew out of the worker's monstrous arms, and I think they were actually surprised.

The struggle between beasts had begun.

Fresh air slapped my face; I came awake; I came alive. I tumbled over the swarming crowd below, stumbling over backs and heads. My legs, swollen and rigid, protested the sudden activity, but I ignored their pleas for rest and blundered about in mad happiness. I knew very well the uproarious shouts behind me were intent to curtail my freedom, but in my delirious delight, I felt the workers were cheering for me.

A monster stood ahead of me, eyes aflame with stress. Their body was upright, and stronger than mine, but I was faster, and I had more to lose. I evaded his grasp; his hands just missed my neck. My body begged for rest, but there would only be running that day. I would either die running or die from not running, and it was obvious which option I would choose.

I threw my face to the sun, for a moment overwhelmed by its glorious warmth. Then I was back on the run. The demons lacked agility, and I used this to my advantage. I darted and dove, and eventually put some method to my madness. My eyes—and heart—sought the exit. Then I saw it: a large, metal gate, with just enough space for me to squeeze through.

Victory was a dash away.

The voices behind me were no longer of consequence. My mind was geared towards one goal.

The gate was open, inviting me forward.

My head burst with panic and joy.

I threw my body over the threshold, and bounded away into a brand new universe.

Discovery would come later. All that mattered was making as much space between me and my enemies as possible. This was the only way I could fight: by running. My lungs burned; my vision swam with stress. These physical exploits made me realize how sick I really was.

Despite my handicaps, rest would have to wait. Though I'd thwarted the monsters for now, I had no idea of knowing how fast they could overtake me. Were they not bloodthirsty? Would they not be hellbent on retrieving their lost prey?

I sometimes slowed to a trot, but ran whenever I could. No matter what, I kept moving.

I was exhausted, yet removed from all limitations. Who knew Nirvana would bring with it such desperation.

Still, there was much to be grateful for. There was a sky above me, not a ceiling. There was ground beneath me, not a floor.

There was clean air, bright sun.

I'd escaped.

I was free.

5 : HELP

How long would I have to run?

When could I rest?

Perhaps forever; maybe never.

Though my body was bred to be consumed, I had a child's mind when assigned to slaughter. I was ignorant of how far my legs could take me, or when I would collapse. Direction, distance—unknown factors! They were never necessary before. What need had I for space when I'd grown up in a dirty pen?

Thoughts were absent. That, or there were too many to make sense of. For oh, freedom! What a word! What a better experience.

It was impossible to concentrate with all that gorgeous air on my face. The wind was soft and clear. It sprayed rocks in my eyes, but it was beautiful all the same! This was my first taste of fresh, unsullied air, and I adored it. I wanted my whole family to feel such a pleasant rush in their lungs.

And the sun! The sky! I didn't know their names yet, but I knew they were perfection.

Adrenaline puckered my veins. The world was wide and vast. Before my escape, I'd only known stingy air and stiff concrete. That and my dreams. But my dreams could never compare to this. There was so much room! I could never have foreseen the infinite sky, its intense deposits of purple and pink. So many miracles whooshed past me as I ran.

To live and live well. To breathe and not cough. The beauty beat me tenderly, rendering me paralyzed. Despite that, I had to run.

And the colours! They were lovely to my irises. That bright, floral splash up above, and that endless array of gold and brown flanking me. What liberty in space, what glee in movement! Enough room for thousands of us to roam free! Why were we kept in captivity? Why were we banished from this paradise?

Traversing this wide open terrain was almost too much to handle. It broke me into tiny shreds of rapture and remorse.

I'd achieved the impossible: the freedom everyone had assured me was unattainable. I'd looked death in the face and beaten it down, just as I'd beaten down whispers of despair and the threat of insanity. It was an admirable feat, but a lonely one. Now that I was bounding through this alien world, I had more questions to answer.

Even as I tumbled down the dusty path, my mind burst.

I saw no trace of the monsters outdoors. Perhaps they too confined themselves to steel walls, but by choice. Perhaps they had no love for these rolling fields of tall, gold plants. If this was true, I would have nothing to fear.

What of the future? I'd had nothing but wistful wonders of escape. My mantra promising evasion had felt like another fairytale my mother told me. I had no thought of what would happen if I actually succeeded!

Where would I go? How could I live out the rest of my days?

Would I find someone who loved me like my mother did?

What did I think would happen after scrambling through that gate? Did I think I'd have a home waiting for me right there?

You can't blame me: I'm a dreamer! Dreamers always venture beyond reality's borders. Dreamers are always a stranger to practicality.

Now I was left to consequences. I was free with nowhere to go. The monsters had shown me nothing closer to love, but they gave me shelter, water, nourishment. Left to my own devices, I was hopeless.

Deflated, I welcomed the dust. Finally I breathed at a normal pace. My brain was pulled from the tides of fight and flight and fight again. The waters ebbed. My pulse slowed.

I had altered the path promised me. I said No to fate, and Yes to destiny.

If only the others had come with me.

I kept walking—though of course, I crawled. I looked up to the infinite, airy dome above me, and knew deep in my soul something so perfect couldn't have been made by the monsters who raised me. Unlike the bright, harsh ceilings, the sky did not confine me.

Being right was bittersweet. I was the only one to escape, to see the sky, to find life behind death. Was I the last of my kind? Would I never see another animal like me again? I didn't even know what I was called!

I wanted someone to share my joy with. For my mother to feel the sun on my cheek.

The longer I walked, the more the atmosphere changed. There was much more to the world than cages! The luminescence in the sky faded, and the ground became darker and rougher to walk on. The tall, gold stalks lessened, soon replaced by strange, square structures that attacked the skyline. They reminded me of the slaughterhouse. Would I be trapped once more?

I continued to crave the most elusive of pleasures: a gentle surface, a place of true repose. Paradise had nothing to offer- yet.

I turned a corner, and that's when I saw it.

What was it? It was hard to tell. It reminded me a lot of my brothers and sisters, except it had fur on its face, and though hunched over, stood on its two feet. It was thinner than me by far, but longer, with sharper teeth. It sniffed, then advanced towards me. I galloped away, and could hear from the creature's grunts that it was in hot pursuit.

Running was too much. That day I had moved more than I could have fathomed. I'd seen more land, witnessed more beauty, and uncovered more horror than anyone could endure.

Again I collapsed, skidding on hard ground.

Had I so narrowly avoided death, only to be met with the same fate so soon? I braced myself for the terrible blow, but it never came. Instead, the thing breathed into my ear and poked me!

I'd only known gentleness from my mother. It almost disturbed me more than violence.

"Come on! It's no fun chasing you if you don't run!"

I scrambled to find distance between myself and this source of smelly breath. He had two eyes in the centre of his face, like me, and a nose like mine, though his was less squished. I could have called him a cousin were it not for his hairy face and fangs.

"Well, come on!" it urged. "Wasn't that fun?"

"No!" I huffed.

"Oh. Fine then," he drooped, but only for a moment. "Where did you come from?"

"Where did you come from?" I shot back, distrustful.

"My home. Sometimes they let me run outside."

"Home? Home exists?"

"Of course!"

I felt nostalgic for a world I'd never known. In another life, would I have been this careless and carefree?

He poked me again.

"You okay? You're bleeding. Almost makes me want to…well, lucky it's not a Full Moon!" he laughed, then he howled. "Say, stand up! Tell me what you are and where you come from!"

"I don't know what I am," I admitted. "I only know I am what my mother was."

He laughed.

"How can you not know what you are?"

"Well, what are you?"

"Me? I'm a werewolf!"

I didn't know what that was, and didn't bother to ask. All I knew was he was nothing like the monsters who had held me captive.

"Do you know what I am?"

"Hmm," he poked me again. "I think so. I think you're a human!"

Human? I stared down at my weak, pink hands. Was that what I was?

The werewolf encouraged me to stand on my two back feet, but I had never stood upright before, and fell yet again. The mutilations of my past would not so easily recede.

A terrible noise shot through the darkness. The monsters! They'd found me! I huddled behind a shiny box until the sound passed us by.

"Don't be scared," the werewolf pulled me out into the open. "They use those pods to move around."

I remembered that rumbling monster the workers had tried to throw me in. Did they use those for travel as well?

My dreams had come true, but I couldn't be certain if the nightmare had ceased.

"What's your story?" he asked again. "Why are you so scared?"

"I had to escape!" I confessed. "The monsters were trying to kill me."

He perked his ears.

"Monsters? What monsters? Want me to get them?"

"Are they out here? They're big and have five arms and five eyes and wear big, metal boots and use tools and..."

He squinted.

"No, no, no. You're not talking about monsters. You're talking about Zenizens! They rule this land. They take care of me!"

"No, no, no. These monsters wouldn't take care of anyone! They tried to kill me! They try to kill everyone!"

"We must be talking about different things."

"I don't think we are. They must treat you differently, that's all." I could scarcely comprehend it, "They're nice to you?"

"Very! They take me for walks and feed me meat and teach me not to get too violent on the Full Moon. Zenizens love werwolves! They say they rescued some of us from a terrible planet, many moons ago. Say, maybe they rescued you, too!"

"I told you," I was convinced, "they would never rescue me! They breed my kind for meat!"

The werewolf frowned.

"That doesn't sound good. I mean, I like human meat, but I never thought too much about where it came from."

"What did you call them?"

"Zenizens!"

Even the shadows had names.

"And they've never tried to kill you?"

"Goodness, no! They treat me like one of the family!"

We were quiet then, unsettled by the truth. Werewolves and humans were, by our approximations, equal in intelligence and build (in fact, if anything, I was the brighter of the two), yet these Zenizens treated one group with hostility and the other with a somewhat patronizing compassion.

The werewolf remained bewildered.

"They don't love you?"

"They don't try to kill you?" I was paralyzed by the concept. A Zenizen capable of love was inconceivable.

I considered my precarious new friendship with this creature. Was it too cruel to educate him further? Yet I could not ignore all I'd witnessed, and unlike the Zenizens, he understood my speech. How could I allow another innocent animal to walk around unawares? Who knows? Perhaps in some places, werewolves were treated just as humans were. If that were so, my new friend may remain vulnerable in his ignorance. If I were to tell the truth, I had to tell all of it.

So I related my morbid tale. He was appalled. He explained that, barring their monthly bloodlust, werewolves were loving animals, and he hated the thought of something as meek as a human suffering so. We repeatedly compared descriptions and had to conclude that the creatures I had feared were the same species he adored. I hated to shatter his dream, but it was a dream that needed shattering.

Who wants to learn that someone who loves them is capable of hate?

It took him a while to digest this information. Finally, he confirmed, "So, you escaped?"

I was moved by his willingness to trust my story so quickly.

"Yes—but what now? I don't know this place, where anything is, and what I really want most is to see my mother again."

"Hmm," he considered, then reconsidered, then suggested, "Let's walk. I think better when I'm walking."

I smiled at that—pacing had helped me think for countless nights in captivity. We shared yet another similarity, yet our experience with the Zenizens was dark and light.

I placed blind confidence in my newly discovered confidant and followed him down dark roads. A companion with ambiguous intention was better than an enemy, or worse, having no one at all.

The werewolf walked on his hind legs, but was equally happy to remain on his hands and knees with me, to keep my pace, and keep me company. To think this creature had lived in comfort in a whole household of Zenizens. Zenizens who, according to him, pet him, fed him, cuddled him (cuddled him!), gave him space to play. Zenizens who loved him.

I wondered what it felt like to receive affection from a Zenizen.

We'd been walking a while when I stalled in my tracks. The werewolf asked me why, but I couldn't answer: my voice was stolen.

Off the side of the road was a patch of colour. It filled my brain like a basin.

The hue was green. Its surface was etched.

I felt my first patch of grass like a blind man. With a little wonder, and a lot of caution, I pressed my palms against its edge, careful not to crush my hopes in case I was being teased by a mirage. Grass was my first glimpse of home.

I threw myself onto the grassy bed and wriggled in glee. It was even softer than I'd imagined, sweeter than I dreamed! But the smell was the same.

My feet kicked the clouds. I knew I looked silly, but I didn't care. Who cares what you look like when you surrender to happiness? That moment would have been perfect if only my family had been there.

The werewolf understood enough to leave me undisturbed in my revelry.

Only after I calmed myself and returned to his side did he say, "So…is this the first time you've seen grass?"

6: HARDSHIP

It was only after I left the grass I noticed the blood on my legs and face. It had begun to flake and rub off my skin. That ball of light in the sky had receded into indigo with little sparkles composing its surface. Its beauty made the blood all the more grotesque. Like the aggressive architecture (which the werewolf called "living pods," which was where the Zenizens slept) ruined the horizon, the blood blemished the grass that had so soothed me.

The ugly facts were intent to bombard me. Even in the midst of the sweetest things, misery would return to haunt me. That blood was reminiscent of the fate that had almost befallen me, and surely ensnared my former friends.

By now, the werewolf was accustomed to my dismal countenance, but he still inquired concernedly, "What's wrong?"

I pushed my head up to the sky. Up there, it was quiet.

"I'll be fine. Thank you. If you could help me somewhat more…"

"Of course!"

"I have to find a place to call home."

"Home! Yes! Where it's warm."

He stiffened, then bounded away without a word of explanation. Only after realizing I had yet to follow him did he return to explain what he presumed an elating prospect, "Why don't you come home with me?"

The notion hit me like a strike on the cheek.

"But you have Zenizens there!" I curled back up on the green grass, half-hoping it would swallow me whole. "Zenizens don't like humans. They tried to kill me."

"It can't be as simple as all that!" the werewolf countered me and countered me well. "My Zenizens love me. And you're my friend! Maybe they'll love you too. They could take care of you like they take care of me, and then everything'll be okay!"

Was I stupid, or desperate? I suppose it looks the same. The idea of being treated well—treated right—was too delicious to abandon just yet.

"Alright then. I'm willing to give it a try. Thank you, werewolf. You have a very kind spirit."

"You too!"

He shoved me in play, wiggled in levity, and scattered off. Two times he had to round back to ensure he hadn't left me behind. I appreciated his concern, yet the gnawing feeling that he was leading me deeper and deeper into a sinister cage made was a tough sensation to shake. Would this journey only end in the hands of Zenizens? Would those hands ever show me love and care?

I tried to trust. I aimed for hope. Others may have given up long ago, and yes, that may have been more logical, but I had no sobriety of the soul. My heart was too big, my dreams too real. I was forever drunk on possibility.

Peace was elementary. Happiness just made sense. Misery, blood, vice, and hatred were senseless.

I continued to cogitate as we walked, the werewolf some feet ahead. He cared little for gazing up at the clouds, but I couldn't take my eyes off them. Why would I busy myself with spots on the ground or smells on a fence when there was a whole universe up above?

Oh, that breathtaking night! It inspired all I'd ever longed to feel. Urges to dazzle and express, dance and parade, learn and teach. Perhaps I could spread the story of my kind. I could show Zenizens that humans were sentient beings worthy of care and consideration. To be shown kindness by a grim, gruff Zenizen—what a dazzling thought! To be held but not restrained, nudged but not kicked, loved and not neglected. Perhaps the werewolf's owner would understand my cries, and bridge the communication between the oppressed and the oppressor. Was it possible? Wasn't anything?

I lost speed, wary of the future, tired with hunger. My recent exploits left me hollow.

Thankfully, we reached the werewolf's Home. I was too famished to fear the Zenizens. He opened the gate, and ushered me inside.

"This is it. My backyard!" proudly, the werewolf displayed the scene. Though he hardly emphasized the space with humility, I couldn't help but be impressed.

"So much grass!"

The werewolf exhaled, content as any animal could be.

"I like it here. It's Home."

So these Zenizens really had given him a Home. A Home he loved, a Home they shared.

Maybe these were different Zenizens, kind Zenizens, the last who cared for animals other than themselves. My heart skipped with longing and anticipation. Suppose they did welcome me as they had my furry companion!

A light spilled onto the grass. It flickered, and my eyes took time to adjust. It should have comforted me, but instead I felt exposed.

"Calm down," I told myself, rejecting the tremble in my throat. *These Zenizens will take care of you. Don't be scared.*

Even after learning the ugly truth, my friend was confident his owners were unlike the others. He genuinely believed they would take care of me like they took care of him. I believed it, too.

"My Zenizen's coming!" he barked.

A shadow cast over us both: a long, large shadow. Like a flash, I fell back to the horrible hell I'd grown up in. The smells. The screeches. The sawing of my teeth. The searing pain between my legs. Every inch of me wanted me to run.

Ignoring my instincts, I spoke, "Sir, sir, might you help me?" I tried to look past its terrible eyes and arms. "I'm hungry and tired and have only just narrowly escaped…"

Like the others, this Zenizen was deaf to me. His mouth moved, eyes contorted.

I was so dizzy with fear, I only caught fragments of his speech.

"What… human… slaughter…"

I turned and ran. My retreat was involuntary, and once I was lost in those same alleyways, I felt like a fool. When the werewolf caught up with me, I prepared to be chastised.

Instead, he urged me with wide, fearsome eyes, "Faster! Faster! He said he was going to take you back that place!"

My heart fell.

"Are you certain?"

"Go, go!" he whimpered. "He sent me to track you down. I'll just go back and pretend I couldn't find you."

From the urgency in his voice, and the shame in his eyes, all my questions were answered. Though Zenizens loved this werewolf as a pet, such affection would not be transferred to me. Zenizens would only ever see me as meat.

Despite this perilous revelation, my feet were rooted.

"Why should I run? If your Zenizen wants me dead, there can't be a single one who wants me alive!"

"You should always run! Run until you can't! Please run, please!"

"What's the point?"

"Listen," he snarled. "I'll chase you if I have to."

I found some strength to smile.

"Thank you."

I parted from yet another friend.

Cruelty confused me. Injustice appeared to grow as freely in the world as grass did.

I was so tired of running every step, fighting for every inch of my life. How could I beat down these insurmountable odds?

I looked at the sky for answers, and of course there were none.

The werewolf was right: I had to run. I'd come this far and had to continue. I had no choice as to when I would or wouldn't die. I could only live as much as I could before my time was up.

What of the Zenizens? What were they capable of? How much of this world did they dominate? Was there another world out there that humans ruled instead? Would that place be any better than this?

I could only hope that if I encountered another Zenizen, they would be more like a human. Or at least, love me like they loved their werewolves.

7: HAPPINESS

I must have fallen asleep, for I was waking up. There had been no dreams: only fatigue and darkness.

Something held me.

Hands.

Zenizen hands!!!

I screamed, but was too tired to run. If they were to have me, let them come! I'd done all I could. I was done.

Much to my shock, surprise, and suspicion, the Zenizen before me did nothing to force me to sit still. Instead, she held out three of her five arms to stroke me, and shush me as she did so. She didn't sound annoyed, but caring, and careful.

When she knelt closer, I saw her eyes. Calm emanated from them. Somehow, with her temperate demeanour and poetic stance, this Zenizen reminded me of a human. She was even down on her knees, face nearly level with my own. She was of course much bigger than me, but I was less concerned. It was her eyes, I think. They sparkled like stars of distant planets.

"Shh, it's alright," she cooed in their native tongue. "See? I'm not going to hurt you. Oh, you poor thing! What have you been through?"

She wrapped something fuzzy around me; it was like portable grass! She gave me water, and fed me from two of her hands. I at first tentatively, then eagerly devoured her offerings. I worried she had a mind to fatten me up, but was too hungry to stop.

All the time I waited for the other boot to fall. When would she grab me, hit me, stomp in her big metal boots to remind me who was boss? Yet, as I lapped up at the water, she made no move of assault. I chomped down the food niblets, and she still rubbed my back.

Gulping, glugging, slurping, dribbling, I was drenched in gratitude. Even if this Zenizen were to betray me later, I would always appreciate the kindness she had first shown.

"Don't worry, little fella," she promised, "We're gonna get you help."

She reminded me of my mother. I inhaled all the food she had to give, and soon all the pats too. I loved how she rubbed my hair, scratched my ear, and let me rest in her lap. The longer she stayed, the more relaxed I became. She hadn't hit me, or yell, and seemed genuinely concerned for my wellbeing. This Zenizen's heart was warm as my own.

She stayed until the others arrived. Surrounded by that many Zenizens, I again froze in fear, and again I was comforted. Would these Zenizens continue her acts of kindness?

This time, my hope came through.

"Hey, sweet thing! How are you?" the tall Zenizen addressed the one who had given me food, "Debanyah, right? Thanks for channelling us over."

"I didn't really know what else to do, you know?"

Other Zenizen hands explored me, and I resisted my urge to flinch, to run, to scream.

"I don't even know where he came from." my rescuer continued. "I know there's processing plants some hyperspecs from here, but I've never heard of humans being raised in the city."

"Oh, he's definitely an escapee," assured one. "Thanks for calling us. You saved this little guy's life! Can you help us get him into the back seat? We'll have him checked out right away by the healer at the sanctuary."

They persuaded, cooed, baited, and finally loaded me into another machine that didn't seem to growl, but purr. The inside of it was soft; there were blankets laid out everywhere for me. They were sure to tuck me in and make sure I wasn't scared.

What was happening? What change was coming upon me? How could I know this change would actually be for the better? If it had been explained to me that I was rescued, that I was to be taken to a place where I was cherished and respected, I may not have been able to believe it. I may not have been prepared for the wonderful truth of dreams coming true.

At the time, my mild confusion was diluted with oblivion. I nuzzled in the blankety fuzz, and soon rested my head on the lap of the tall one. He was thick-scaled, like all male Zenizens, but had some fuzz on his face, which reminded me of my werewolf friend.

I fell asleep again, rested in the arms of a Zenizen, unafraid.

I knew nothing of our destination. I was more lost in that transport pod that I'd been on the streets. Somehow I knew they weren't taking me to slaughter. It was just a feeling—but a strong one.

There were Zenizens who cared, who could rise above the hurt and be instruments for good.

When we arrived, they encouraged me to stand upright, and I of course failed. They comforted me, and carried me off. The last time I was heaped into a Zenizen's many arms, I had resisted with all my might. Now, I felt taken care of.

The effulgence of the day reached an inspiring peak. I thought of the home I'd never had, the mother I'd been torn from too soon. I caught glimpses off a stream, tall bales of that gold plant, and grass. So much grass! I was in a land of forever rolling hills. All was alive and green.

The grass and sky conferred to me the perfect image of peace. Perhaps on the other side of death, everyone found a paradise like this.

Many Zenizens held me that day. I was weighed, bandaged, cuddled, and kissed. There were hands that pricked me with needles, tamed my hair, massaged my weary bones.

Then, they showed me my Home.

There were other humans there: some who had escaped from slaughterhouses, and a few that had been humanely bred. We exchanged stories, and expressed our gratitude at no longer being alone.

All of us carried our past in our hearts, but our minds were on the future. These Zenizens couldn't understand our language, either, but they recognized our consciousness. They saw we could feel pain, love, fear, anger. They knew we deserved food and sleep and space to play.

At the sanctuary, I could roll on the grass without bumping into anyone. There was always food, water, and a Zenizen nearby to pet me. In these rolling hills, I never saw a hint of abuse, nor did I ever see another creature writhing in pain or dying from neglect.

I'd gone from being treated as a piece of machinery—a product to be butchered and sold—to being treated for who I am: a living, breathing soul.

Some of the older humans corroborate what my werewolf friend said: the Zenizens did visit our old planet, and steal some of us to breed for meat. That was a long time, ago, though. So long ago it is likely mythology.

It doesn't matter. I'm happy here. I have learned that trust is reasonable, love is eternal, and hope is never a waste of time.

The Zenizens give us music and paint. They encourage me to dance and speak, though they can't understand me. But perhaps one day they will.

If I learn to speak like them, or they learn to hear me, maybe one of them will be able to sit down and tell my story.

Stories like mine deserve to be heard.

AFTERWORD: HEARKEN

TELESCONIC DATA EXCERPT:

HUMAN RESCUE SOCIETY:

LOG V#$%^&S:

A male human was found bruised, exhausted, and splattered in blood outside a Zenizen's living pod in (urban site withheld). After ensuring it was alive, the citizen channeled our team down to pick up the terrified creature. We have since named him Hearken, and he has adjusted well to his new home.

Hearken is a human who has beaten all the odds. He was raised for meat in a slaughterhouse, as evidenced by his filed down teeth and absence of testicles (likely removed without anesthetic). During transport to slaughter, Hearken managed to escape, and was found to be suffering from fatigue and pneumonia (a human disease related to their only having two lungs). After physical and emotional rehabilitation, Hearken has proven to be a sturdy fellow with a love for watching the clouds and rolling around in the grass. He has snuggled his way into our hearts and is one of our favourite animals here at the sanctuary.

We hope Hearken's story will continue to illuminate the abuse in slaughterhouses and inspire more Zenizens to avoid consumption of human meat.

Though friendly with all creatures, Hearken prefers the company of other humans, and, interestingly, werewolves.

Notes on Previous Publications

Many thanks to those who gave my misfit toys an island!

First Date #5- Schlock! UK Webzine

B&E- Black Lantern Magazine

Cobwebs (published as A Friend, The Spider)- Arcane Magazine

Adam's Apples- Space Squid Magazine

Get Away From That Car- Sage Cigarettes

Schrodinger's Cats- Ergi Press

Beauty vs Beast- Suburban Witchcraft Magazine

Vibrationis Vibrissae- Silver Honourable Mention in the L Ron Hubbard Writers of the Future Contest 2022

Acknowledgements

269

Thank you lovers, bullies, family and friends.

Thank you to my editor, publisher, test readers.

Thank you to the Alberta Foundation for the Arts for their generous grant!

Thank you Margaret Keene for your endless encouragement; I am eternally grateful and incredibly sad that you passed on before you could read this.

Thank you Uncle Deryk for your kindness and sweetness; same as above.

Grateful acknowledgement to the First Nation Peoples whose land this was written on, including but not limited to the Blackfoot and Cree.

Thank you analysts, therapists, Universe.

Most of all, thank YOU, reader.

Thanks for being here.

Loved the book? Give it five stars on Goodreads!

Find more weirdness at cehoffman.net

Follow C on Twitter @CEHoffman2

"Do you ever think that life is a game of musical chairs, and the music stopped, and we're the only ones without a chair?"

"All the time."

—Xander, Willow, *Buffy the Vampire Slayer*